Charles F. Forshaw

A Legend of St. Bees

and other poems

Charles F. Forshaw

A Legend of St. Bees
and other poems

ISBN/EAN: 9783337391300

Printed in Europe, USA, Canada, Australia, Japan

Cover: Foto ©Andreas Hilbeck / pixelio.de

More available books at **www.hansebooks.com**

A LEGEND

OF

ST. BEES:

AND OTHER POEMS.

BY

CHAS. F. FORSHAW, LL.D.

HONORARY DOCTOR OF DENTAL SURGERY OF THE BALTIMORE COLLEGE OF DENTAL SURGERY.

AUTHOR OF "WANDERINGS OF IMAGERY," "THOUGHTS IN THE GLOAMING," "POEMS," ETC., ETC.

London:

SIMPKIN, MARSHALL, HAMILTON, KENT & CO.,
PATERNOSTER ROW.

Bradford:

THORNTON & PEARSON.   G. B. RUSSELL.

Enniskillen: Saint Bees:

TRIMBLE.   R. W. BROOMFIELD

Malton:

G. J. JONES.

AUTHOR'S PREFACE.

— ❦ —

THE Author has received the names of several hundred subscribers who ordered copies of this work prior to its publication. Amongst these he may mention His Grace the Duke of Devonshire, H. I. Butterfield, Esq., of Cliffe Castle, Keighley, Sir Edwin Saunders, F.R.C.S., Dental Surgeon to Her Majesty the Queen, Sir Henry Mitchell, J.P., Sir James Bain, M.P. for Whitehaven, Hy. Byron Reed, Esq., M.P., His Worship Councillor Hammond, J.P., Mayor of Bradford, George Ackroyd, Esq., J.P., Arthur Briggs, Esq., J.P., W. Anderton, Esq., J.P., and W. J. Kaye, Esq., M.A., Principal of Ilkley College.

Over one hundred Clergymen who have attended the Theological course at St. Bees also sent in their names for copies, and amongst these are the Rev. Canon Knowles, M.A., Principal of the College, the Rev. Canon Woodhouse, M.A. (late Lecturer), and other well known clerical gentlemen. To these and all other supporters of the volume the Author tends his sincere thanks.

CHAS. F. FORSHAW.

WINDER HOUSE, MANNINGHAM LANE,
BRADFORD, August, 1891.

PUBLISHERS' PREFACE.

—➤o◄—

IN introducing this volume to the notice of the public, the publishers have thought it desirable to give some account of the Author's career. They, therefore, reproduce the accompanying article culled from the columns of that excellent weekly "The Leeds Mercury Supplement."

DR. CHARLES F. FORSHAW, M.A. LL.D. &c., &c., is one of the most promising of the younger poets of Yorkshire. His name although now mainly local, will, if we mistake not, take rank among the sweet singers of England in a much broader sense. He was born at Bilston, in Staffordshire, on January 23rd, 1863, the son of Mr. T. G. Forshaw, and grandson of the Rev. Thurstan Forshaw, Vicar of Newchapel, Staffordshire, for thirty-five years, and seems to have inherited his talent for poesy from his great-uncle, the Rev. Thos. Garratt, M.A. Vicar of Audley, Staffordshire, who published a volume of poems in 1818, which had an extensive sale. Although not born in Yorkshire, Dr. Forshaw has spent the greater portion of his life in the county, having come to Bradford when quite young (in 1864) with his father, who had obtained the appointment of dispenser of medicine to the Bradford Infirmary and Dispensary, and there he was educated. Brought up as a chemist and dentist, he commenced the profession of dentistry, and was the founder, and is now the senior surgeon, of the Bradford Dental Hospital, he is also the Honorary Dental Surgeon of the Bradford Tradesmen's Home, and the Nutter Orphanage ; late Dentist to the Bradford Children's Hospital, and Consulting Dentist to Ilkley College. In 1885 he had conferred on him the diploma of doctor of dental surgery; he is an Honorary Member of the British and Foreign Association, and a short time ago Sir H. Trueman Wood, M.A. the Secretary of the Society of Arts, asked him to join that old and honoured body; besides which he has been elected a member of the Society of Chemical Industry; a Fellow of the Royal Microscopical Society, London, the Geological Society, Edinburgh, and of several other learned and scientific societies, including that of Science, of London, by which he was awarded a year or two ago, the gold medal of merit. He is also the inventor and patentee of two or three medical and surgical appliances, which have met with universal approbation from the faculty, both in England and America, and in recognition of these he has received gold medals and certificates. But it is as a poet, scientific writer, and popular lecturer that Dr. Forshaw is best known and most entitled to distinction : his poems, charming by their sweetness, melody, and purity of senti- ment, are scattered over many journals. His published volumes are "Wanderings of Immagery," "Thoughts in the Gloaming," and "Poems" the later just from the press. His scientific works are on "Stammering," "The Teeth," "Alcohol," and "Tobacco." Dr. Forshaw in 1884 married Miss Mary Elizabeth James, of Rouch Farm, Stoke- upon-Trent.

We offer no apology for inserting the portrait of Dr. Forshaw, which has been executed by one of the leading artists of the day—T. Tindall Wildridge, Esq., of Hull— and for quoting the several poetical tributes at the end of the volume. These have been written by poets' in almost every walk of life, and though greatly differing in poetical merit are given to show the admiration and respect in which Dr. Forshaw is held by his brother bards.

THE PUBLISHERS.

17, BARKEREND ROAD,
    BRADFORD, August, 1891.

CONTENTS.

TO THE

SPIRIT OF POESY.

INVOCATION

TO THE SPIRIT OF POESY.

—————

THRICE blessed Spirit, I would have thine aid,
　　And would invoke thee in mellifluous strains!
I my rapt soul unburden to thine ear;
List then, oh list, and come at my bequest.
I, thine unworthy servant, lift my voice
And pour my heart's wish forth in clarion tones;
Albeit my language comes in feeble words,—
Should'st thou descend unto my longing brain
My everlasting blessings shall be thine.

I would not woo thee with a coward soul,
For all in all thou'st ever been to me;
But I would woo thee with a burning tongue
Until thou gav'st me all thine eloquence.
I ne'er yet found thee wanting when I called!
My wishes unto thee were scarce made known
Ere thy sweet gifts were showered freely down;
And I fear not that NOW thou'lt visit me,
And lend me for a season gifts divine.

E'en while I ask I feel my pulses thrill
With tenfold joy, with madd'ning ecstasy!
Therefore I know that all thy pregnant charms
For a brief season unto me belong.
So, lovely being! Borne along by thee
I tread th' enchanted groves of poesy.

A LEGEND OF ST. BEES.

―――

"And oft conducted by historic truth,
We tread the long extent of backward time."

―――

GO back, old Time; go back twelve hundred years,
    And let me see what thou wast doing then
On the sea coast of rock-bound Cumberland?
Obedient to my wish, Time stops his race,
His wheel turns back, and, lo! he places me
In the dim years of the forgotten past.

Like a demoniac gloating in his wrath,
    And glutted with a fiend's desire to slay,
The lightning's flash swept madly o'er the earth
    Causing destruction, danger, and dismay.

Oh! thou magnificent and splendid power,
Thou art the wonder of the universe,
Thou fill'st all hearts with terror and with dread,
And makes amazement stand upon our brow,
Whilst fear stamps us as creatures insignificant.
Thou art, indeed, sublimely grand, but awe
From us, takes thy sublimity away,
And leaves us poor, hopeless, wretched mortals.
Thy vivid, fiery dart, the thunder's roll,
Tell of thy might, and make us cringe beneath
The fury of the storm.

         Another streak
Hangs for a moment in mid-air and then
Vanishes for ever.

         Ah! now a clap
Falls with redoubled energy, gathering
A concentrated force; but horror now
Is giving way to thoughtfulness, as we
Think of the One Supreme, who e'er controls
This dread-inspiring element.

And though
A flash once more illumes the darkened air,
'Tis lost at once in earth's wide wilderness :
Now it is followed by vast, roaring peals
From the huge artillery of Heaven,
Yet feel we not afraid, although our hearts
Beat with tumultuous motion as we
Think of the frailness of our storm-tossed world.

Thy forkéd tongue tells us of God's promise,
The heavy rain now pouring torrents down
Makes memory once more clear, and reminds us
That by it, the earth, shall ne'er more be destroyed.

Thou art a truly great and noble spectacle,
Astounding in thy beauteous majesty.

Wildly the wind blew round Whitehaven's coast,
Lashing the waves to fury in its wrath ;
A little barque, nigh driven to its doom,
By the sore tossings of the tempest stern,
Sought refuge in the harbour close at hand.

On board the ship with many sisters dear
Journeyed a lady abbess, great and good;
Their time, their all, devoted to the laud
And worship of the King of all the world.
When safely landed on Whitehaven's shore,
Secure from being engulphed beneath the wave,
They sped a prayer unto their Lord Supreme,
Thanking Him for their safe deliverance,
And for the preservation of their lives.
But how dismayed each heart, benumbed each brain,
When, looking towards the bay that sheltered them,
They found the hungry waters had destroyed
Their ship, their chattels, all that it contained,
Leaving them strangers in a foreign land,
Without the means of sustenance—no roof
To cover their devoted heads, and none,
No none to give relief.

                    Did I say none?
If so, methinks for once my hasty pen
Well nigh led me astray; for He above
Has ne'er yet seen the destitute forsaken
But He has sent them—if they trusted Him,

Hope, comfort, succour, and the means to live.
And so in this their tribulation's hour,
He led their footsteps up to Egremont,
The castle of the lord of all the land
For many miles around.

A godly woman
Had long been mistress of that mansion strong,
And when they came to her with prayers and tears,
She "pitied their distress," and to each one
Extended that sweet blessing "sympathy."

IT comes from realms of lasting day,
　　Through golden archways bright;
It comes from the home of blisses,
　　From the shore of dazzling light.

'Tis cherished by all the angels,
　　And nursed by that holy throng;
'Tis loved by mortals here below,
　　With a love both pure and strong.

A treasure sent from God above
　　To His children upon earth,
To soothe them in affliction's hour,
　　By the power that gave them birth !

It comes from lands of joy and peace,
　　Where grim sorrow ne'er is known ;
It comes with a Saviour's message,
　　From Heaven's exalted throne.

It speaks with soft and gentle voice,
　　Of our hopes and joys it tells;
It lives within the inner soul,
　　And it there for ever dwells.

　　　　　　　We all know pity
Is akin to love—they who pity, love ;
And love of kind is dearest love of all.
She pitied them, and she prevailed upon
Her lord and master to give unto them
Some place where they might live in peace for aye.

Egremont's lord could never steel his heart
Against the wishes of his lady fair,
He, too, felt love within his bosom glow
For his dear mistress, and he honoured e'er
The slightest favours that she asked.

                                So he,
My lord, unto the homeless gave a home
In the small village of St. Bees, and there
For many years they toiled and spinned and sewed,
And tapestry and carpets made ; living
Such godly lives that made them each by all
Beloved.

                        Congenial were their tasks, they ne'er
Complained, nor murmured at hard fate's decree ;
But hitherto their lives had been for Him,
The Saviour of the universe—alone ;
And oft-times they would raise their voice to Heaven
Saying that if He willed it, would He send
In the near future unto them, a home
Where they could worship Him as they were wont,

Where they could pious live, and do much good
By prayers, solicitations, and advice.

Again the Ruler of earth, sea, and sky
Directed them and told them what to do,
Once more their way they wend to Egremont,
Again they interviewed their mistress kind
And say to her, they long so much to lead
The life which erst they led, before the storm
Deprived them of the means of doing it—
That far and near, all round, they've been beseeched
By many friends to found an Abbey near,
That they would join them in their glorious work,
And to the cause of Truth devote their lives;
Would she, oh! would she pray her noble lord
To build for them a house where they might live
And worship God as they once did of old.

My lady—ever gracious, was most pleased
To ask him their request to gratify—
Oh! how sweet kindness fills the breast with joy
Whene'er her aid for others we employ.

KINDNESS! thou fount of all our bliss,
  Thou blossom from above;
Thy gentle lips for ever kiss
  With pure and lasting love;
Thou mak'st us smile when bathed in tears,
Banishing all our worldly fears.

Kindness! thou art a ray of light,
  A dazzling rainbow, shining
In colours with soft radiance bright,
  A balm to all repining;
Thou turnest darkness into day,
And 'witches all dull care away.

Kindness! thou sunshine of the heart,
  That only springs to life,
And ever dost great strength impart
  To those who're crushed by strife;
Kindness! thou'rt spread from pole to pole,
The solace of the weary soul.

But when my lady went their boon to crave
Of him who owned the land whereon they dwelt
Loud laughed my lord—he was in merry mood

And said, forsooth, what will they long for next?
Ha! Ha! to-morn, said he, will see the day
Of midsummer, and I shall be most glad
To give to them—extending for all time—
Sufficient land to build their Abbey on,
And what is more, I'll build the Abbey too,
If in the morn the land is covered o'er
With snow; nay, but I'll give to them each inch,
Each rood, each acre, where the snow doth fall—
And loud once more he gave a vent to mirth.

The sisters and their abbess sorrowed then,
And for a time distress o'er them held sway,
Yet they did not despair, but comfort found
By faith and trust in God's most holy will,
And sped on high to Heaven this heartfelt prayer:—

FATHER, Supreme! Thy servants kneel
    And earnestly implore
That Thou with us will kindly deal
    As thou hast dealt before.
Oh! touch with all Thy gracious word,
And make him to Thy voice be heard.

Father, Supreme! unto Thy will
  Oh! make him bend beneath,
And he Thy word will then fulfil,
  And to us now bequeath
Sufficient land where we can make
A house to pray in, for Thy sake.

Father, Supreme! Oh! touch his heart
  And then he will relent,
If Thou Thy Spirit dost impart,
  Once more shall knees be bent;
And we to Thee will voice upraise
Swelling an endless song of praise.

Father, Supreme! if in the morn
  Snow covers all the land,
And with its whiteness doth adorn
  The erstwhile golden sand,
Hiding the earth, the grass, the flowers,
Where'er it falleth—that is ours.

Father, Supreme! oh! send the snow;
    He says that he will give
Unto Thy servants here below
    Land and a house to live,
If on the ground to-morn we find
The beauteous snow; O Lord, be kind.

FALL gently down, ye pure, soft flakes of snow,
    Cover the golden sands with garlands bright,
    Deck them in fleecy covering of white;
Make them to wear thy garments spotless glow.

Cast us a myriad feathers here below,
    Each one unsullied—full of glad delight,
    Each one a pearl-gem—lovely, fair, and light;
And when your garb on all has cast its glow,
                        Fall gently down.

Now, when your robe has mantled all the earth,
    Weaved it a dress both beautiful and chaste,
We quite forget our former thoughts of dearth
    For you have with your foliage all things graced.
Oh! still as you bequeath to all new birth,
                        Fall gently down.

When monarch Sol once more lit up the earth
On that bright, merry, leafy morn of June,
My lord from out the castle window high
Did gaze, and lo! as far as he could see
Down to the ocean, and for miles around,
Was covered with the gentle flakes of snow;
Amazement was depicted on his face,
And to his lady hurriedly he hied
To bid her look—to see the wondrous sight.

She said "It is God's will, and we will build
For them an Abbey where in future years
Unto their Maker they may give all praise."

Egremont spoke :

        " My love, it shall be so,
And as I promised, they shall have the land
Which now is covered by the fleecy snow,
The town Whitehaven, too, is also theirs,
The mountains, and the forest Inerdale ;
And all the tithes that to them now belong
Shall be support for St. Bees' Nunnery,

So that, in future years, no scarcity,
No want nor dearth shall these my sisters know.

And thus it was the Abbey of St. Bees
Was founded in those brave old days of yore,
And though Old Time has laid the fabric low.
Traces are left to show to human ken
That all things worldly crumble unto dust;
Pointing the moral that we all should live
For brighter, better, purer realms above,
Where for eternity we ne'er grow old,
Nor wither, nor corrupt, nor fade away,
And where the mansions of the maker—God,
Decay not, like those raised by earthly hands.
All, all is lasting, holy, great and good,
Perfect in form and planned by skill divine:
A home of love, where comes no darksome night
To dull the glories of the long delight.

SONNETS.

TO THE NINE.

—

YE nymphs descend on one who'd be your swain,
    For I can offer you a love whose power
  Would make the heart of bravest mortal cower;
So wild, so strong, so deep, shall be its strain.

If to my eager pleadings ye will deign
    Impart to me a soft, refreshing shower
    Of that sweet essence from your heav'nly bower;
'Tis all I ask—let me not ask in vain.

Lo! as I speak, I hear a voice say,—" Bring
    To this frail mortal that enchanted wine
  Of which one sip will make him freely sing
    With joyous madness that is half divine."

The nymph returns, but in my trembling haste
I drop the chalice ere I've time to taste.

THE SONNET.

I LOVE to be " cribbed, cabined and confined "
   Within the sonnet's fourteen lines of space ;
  To me it seems the ' beau-ideal ' of grace
Into its limits to compress the mind.
Tho' some assert its narrow boundaries bind
   And stop the flow of thought's untiring pace,
   I would not add a line, nor one erase
To mar a feature that the gods designed.

A thing of beauty 'tis, wherein the soul
   Finds blest enchantment, glorious, divine,
   With all the witchery that enthralled the Nine;
No wonder, then, that all its charms extol,—
And that free praise is ever vented on it,
Soft, soothing, sweet, stately, seductive sonnet.

TWO RECTORIES.

—

SNUGLY embosomed 'neath the leafy trees,
   Away from carking care, and sin, and guile,
And each surrounded by fair, fertile leas,
  Two houses stand, on which God loves to smile,
  One in Old England—one in Erin's Isle.
Here dwell my friends, and here I oft have strayed
Holding blest converse with each tuneful maid,
  Converse made sweet by kindred sympathies.

The poet's soul can tremble with delight
  When waves of wild emotion stir his breast;
So has my soul throbbed with o'ermastering might
  And felt the poet's longing and unrest,
And oft at Bulmer and at Derrybrusk,
Poetic pains I've had from early morn till dusk.

GLADSTONE.

A BIRTHDAY GREETING.

—

NO wonder people call thee "Grand Old Man,"
    For age sits lightly on thy noble brow,
And tho' thy years have long since passed their span
    Their heavy cares have scarcely made thee bow.
What matters it, if, differing from thy creed
    We disagree with what thou do'st or say'st ?
Even thy foes reluctantly concede
    Thou only doest what thou thinkest best.
Let us to day then, for a space, forget
    The party feelings and the party strife,
And wish thee ere thy earthly sun may set
    Many more years of blest and happy life,
And pray its winter may be long and bright
Ere flees thy spirit to the Realms of Light.

RUSKIN.

—

MAN of the master mind—the giant brain,
   The heart of oak—the firm, the pow'rful will;
I hail thee, friend, and send to thee this strain
   A tribute to thy genius and thy skill.
Thy works, thy ways, in clarion tones speak out
   And stamp thee sure, a very king of men,
All things to thee are destitute of doubt,
   And no one doubts thy keen far-seeing ken.
Above the hand of steel the velvet glove,
   Beneath thy firmness, kind and gentle ways,
Ways full of love, and ah! thou well can'st love
   With love that's shorn of outwardly displays.
May thy strong pen, so fertile and so bold,
Long write the words that never will grow old.

DEPRESSION.

—

INTO my soul sometimes sad thoughts will creep,
   And fill my bosom with a vague unrest;
   My mind grows weary and I feel depressed,—
Morpheus at night gives no refreshing sleep.

Methinks 'twould ease me if I could but weep;
   Strange sounds my ears, strange sights my eyes infest,
   Until I cry " Why am I so distressed?
Why so cast down with visions dark and deep?"

Night's lonely vigils. long. and dread, and drear,
   In time pass by, and then when comes the morn
   I say " Sure now of grief I shall be shorn;"
But morn alas no comfort bringeth near,
Rather it adds unto my former fear
   And makes me feel more wretched and forlorn.

GLADNESS.

—

ᴺOW my rapt soul awakes to mirth and glee,
　　And fair Thalia's impress, soft, benign,
　Has lent me something of its stamp divine,
Filling my breast with truest gaiety.

Like tuneful joybells, ringing full and free,
　　My spirit seems in all my works to shine ;
　And even now, when wooing the coy Nine,
With peals of laughter come they unto me.

Ripples each vein with madd'ning sense of joy,
　　My thoughts are smiles which come with bound
　　　and start,
　And all my frame shares in their wild impart,
With sweet emotions that have now no cloy
To hinder them, or dull them, or destroy
　　The glad impulses of my inmost heart.

TO GEORGE ACKROYD, ESQ., J.P.

ON HIS SEVENTY-SECOND BIRTHDAY.

I.

ONG before God ordained that I should come
 To this great world of mingled joy and care ;
The tuneful Nine had made thy heart their home
 And crowned thee with their laurels bright and fair.
Seventy long years and two their course have fled,
 But still the nymphs delight to dwell with thee,
For long before thou unto them were wed,
 Thou'dst wooed them well and sought them constantly.
To-day, the sweet, the kind Mnemosyne,
 Came whisp'ring in my ever willing ear,
And bade me write a line or two to thee—
 To whom thou art and ever wilt be dear,
I took my pen to answer her command
And asked her well to guide my falt'ring hand.

II.

Still may the maidens of celestial joy,

    Prove unto thee a mine of fond delight ;

And at thy call, may they be never coy—

    But always answer when thou dost invite.

May their fresh charms increase with rolling years,

    Still may'st thou stray upon their heav'nly Mount,

May their companionship be balm for fears—

    A soul inspiring—heart-rejoicing fount.

May many years of happiness be thine,

    Ere yet thou'rt called to Lands of Lasting Light ;

And may'st thou by God's Holy care Divine,

    Spend all thy earthly days serene and bright,

And in the Golden Realms of Paradise

Spend an eternal birthday in the skies.

AT THE BRIDGE.

SUMMER.

HERE let me rest awhile, and watch the stream
   Merrily flowing 'neath the Summer's sun ;
  How bright and joyous doth it blithely run,
A subject meet for poet's fairest theme.

Pregnant with life—it seems with mirth to teem :
   Its bubblings speak of happiness and fun ;
   Its sparkling, sportive ways are never done,
Bounding along with many a flashing gleam.

How gay the pebbles in its shallow bed !
   How soft and cool the moss upon its shore !
   How quick the fish that dart its waters o'er !
How green the branches waving overhead !

   And oh ! the many-shaded flowers how sweet
   That snugly nestle 'neath the noontide heat.

AT THE BRIDGE.

WINTER.

But lo! the scene hath changed.   King Winter's hand
  Hath stripped the foliage from the once gay trees,
  And 'stead of lightsome wind or zephyr breeze,
Fierce gusts blow harshly over all the land.

How wild the scene! but yet how wildly grand!
  The flowers are gone and barren are the leas,
  And yet we love Queen Nature's mysteries,
And feel that they are well and wisely planned.

Though ice-bound now—the stream will flow again;
  The flowers will bloom—the leaves once more appear;
  The Summer's sun again will shine out clear,
And shed his glory over wood and plain.

  We love the Summer more when we have known
  To list with dread rude Winter's dismal moan.

THE BIRTH OF THE NEW YEAR.

—

AMID the peal of joybells wildly ringing,
   The new year comes in 'majesty and pride ;
   With halcyon brow, with noble, lordly stride,
Heralded in with sound of sweetest singing.

Like the gay lark 'mid fields of corn upspringing,
   Who soars aloft to sing to his young bride ;
   The year looks down on its domain so wide,
Knowing, perhaps, what 'tis to mortals bringing.

God grant our salutation to the year
   May be auspicious of the coming days ;
   May they be bright with harmony and praise
To Him who sends them to His children here.

And may to-day—the first one of its birth,
Give happiness to thousands on the earth.

THE DEATH OF THE OLD YEAR.

THE year we hailed with gladness and delight,
   In a few moments will be sped for aye :
   Mayhap 'tis well ! we would not have it stay,
With all its mingled happiness and blight.

A death-like stillness floats across the night—
   Our thoughts are full of awe, and far away ;
   Our souls seem nigh enthralled and held at bay ;
Our every sense seems struggling 'gainst some might.

How weirdly wan pale Luna's light appears ;
   E'en the faint breeze is hushed and scarce dare sigh;
   The rustling trees are moaning to the sky,
With wailing sob-like sound of pent-up tears.

Then through the sombre dulness, drear and dread,
The wearied year departs with silent tread.

A LONDON FOG.

—

IT kills the air we struggle to inhale,
  This noisome mass of dirt, and damp, and smoke ;
  It hangs around us like a Stygian cloak,
And wraps us in an overwhelming veil.
The slimy vapour—like some monstrous snail—
  Soon doth our garments with its foulness soak ;
  Fiercely it tugs, until we almost choke—
Dauntless is he who does not from it quail.
Men move like spectres, ghastly, gaunt, and grim,
  Enshrouded and enveloped 'mid its maze,
  Shrinking, yet madd'ned at the deadly haze
Which stupefies each sense and numbs each limb.
Happy the man who ne'er yet felt the clog,
The biting thraldom of a London fog.

JUNE.

JUNE comes in all the pride of womanhood,
　　Dress'd in glorious garb of leaves and flowers ;
　　And in ten thousand glens, and meads, and bowers
She graceful reigns—the Empress of each wood.
And ah ! her rule is beautiful and good :
　　She fills the rills with soft refreshing showers ;
　　And gives to us those perfume-laden hours
Which fly too soon from her fair habitude.
Sweet is her breath ! melodious her voice !
　　Stately her form ! yet gentle as the breeze
　　That softly sighs through all her well-clad trees,
Making her children, bird, bud, bee, rejoice.
But radiant, rapturous June will quickly fly,
Leaving her offspring, all forlorn, to die.

THE BRONTËS.

—

TIME in his flight no lustre takes away
 From the great Brontës wide, immortal fame;
 They nobly gained an everlasting name,
Winning the laurels that know no decay.
Their 'scutcheon is undimmed—its glorious ray
 Has ever shone with bright translucent flame;
 So in the future will it shine the same
And be the theme of many a distant day.
The records of the present and the past
 Reveal no history akin to theirs;
They bravely fought against life's fitful blast,
 Still struggling on, amid a myriad cares!
But ere the world could on their talents rave
The cypress wreath was laid upon their grave.

JOHN NICHOLSON.*

—

ɳO feeble intellect was thine—thy strains
    In wildest grandeur were indeed complete;
Succoured and nourished by Elysian rains,
    What wonder then their tunes were ever sweet?
And, when apostrophising thy dear dales,
    Thy words rang out with eloquence divine,
Filling the moorlands and the woods and vales
    With minstrelsy which pen can scarce define.
Nigh half a century has passed away
    Since thou wert called to thine eternal rest;
But thou art not forgotten, and I pay
    To thee this tribute which thy songs suggest;
For on thy county's glory-roll of fame,
Amongst the bards, thine is a foremost name.

---

* Widely known in Yorkshire as "The Airedale Poet."

GWENDOLIN.

—

A DAINTY little maiden, full of grace,
     With nut-brown hair and eyes of clearest blue;
With tender features on a winsome face,
     And every action pure, and sweet, and true.
A blithesome child who yet has known no care—
     Whom earth has sullied with no taint of sin,—
Her every movement gay and debonair
     And suiting well the name of Gwendolin.
Nothing to mar her childhood's happy days—
     Nothing to give a moment's thought of pain—
And nought to dull her merry, prattling ways—
     As, gaily walking in the country lane
She laughs, and romps, and talks with eager glee,
And shares full half her perfect joys with me.

ARTHUR.

—

ONLY a little, crowing, baby boy,
   And yet 'tis bliss to see his whilom fun;
To watch him jump, and start, and scream with joy,
   And kick with zest, although he cannot run.
How glad it is to watch his sparkling eyes
   Gazing with wonderment on things around:
To see their look of innocent surprise
   Fade in a moment to a glance profound.
Lo! now he stretches forth his chubby arms!
   Is it because to me he wants to come?
To let me see his many varied charms
   Which crown him King of this his realm and home?
Sweet, rosy Arthur—cherub of delight,
I'm happier far, for thy gay pranks, to night.

DESTINY.

—

UNFOLD the scroll of time ye learn'd magicians,
    Pourtray to me what in the future lies ;
    Whether my lot will lie 'neath ambient skies,
Fulfilling all my longings and ambitions,
Or if it is besieged by superstitions,
    Surrounded by stern sorrow's sordid sighs,
    Which now my heart rebelliously defies,
And caring nought for such worn-out traditions.
Lo ! the magician's answer, " Youth is wise—
    And recks not of the future or its blight ;
But when age comes their hope too quickly dies,
    Plunging them o'er in gulphs of darkest night.
Then looking back upon life's early scene
They sadly murmur ah ! it might have been."

REMORSE.

—

OH! cruel pangs that haunt me day and night,
　　Begone from me and let me rest in peace;
　　From thy harsh fetters give me kind release
And take from off my soul thy awful blight.
Beneath the power of thine o'erwhelming might,
　　Which never for a moment seems to cease;
　　I'm worn, and bent, and still my woes increase,
For thou alas! wilt grant me no respite.
Insatiate fiend, get gone! I fain would sleep,
　　And for a space thine awful voice forget;
Go hence to regions dismal dark and deep,
　　Nor make me by thy presence longer fret.
Ah! woe is me—and though I cannot weep
　　I hear him whisper, "no! not yet—not yet!"

MIDNIGHT OIL.

—

'TIS true the poet's thoughts come best at night,
  When beast, and bird, and bush are fast asleep;
But all day long come loving thoughts and light
  And he need not his lonely vigils keep.
The coyful muse disdains a time to fix
  When she shall haunt him with her witchery;
Each nymph must come at will with wilful tricks,
  Nor forcéd be to visit constantly.
And when enveloped in her rapturous coil
  He needs no help from puny, feeble man,
Nor waits to light his flask of midnight oil,
  Nor counts each word, lest lines should fail to scan
For when the muse appears, she gives to him
That perfect power which nought on earth can dim.

THE POET'S FIRE.

THERE is a fire within the Poet's heart
    That glows with strong, unvarying, vivid flame,
And, casting forth its bright and beaming dart,
    It puts all thought of sordid things to shame
By its clear light, which flickers not, nor dims,
    All things with radiant lustre seem to shine;
None other hand but his the fuel trims—
    None other voice breathes forth the words divine.
This flame is seen by all—it fiercely burns,
    And yet the world on it forbears to gaze,
Knowing nor feeling half his heartfelt yearns—
    How can it comprehend the poet's ways?
Neglected and unheeded—when he dies
All the world wakes and says 'This man was wise.'

A SUMMER DAY.

I SAT and mused beside a running stream,
  The dancing waters filled my soul with joy—
And shed upon my life a gladsome gleam
  That future cares will never quite destroy.
The month was June, the day was passing fair,
  For Sol shone gaily over wood and lea,
And tinted earth with beauty rich and rare,
  And filled the land with radiancy and glee.
The merry insects flitted to and fro—
  The feathered songsters sang their song of praise,—
The flowers shed their perfume and their glow,
  Amid a scene that artist ne'er pourtrays,
How glad my heart that on this perfect day
The power is mine that where I list I stray.

A BIRTHDAY GREETING.

—

AWAKE! dear Gabrielle! awake and rise!
  This is the morn when first you came to earth,
May many such await with glad surprise
  And welcome still the day that saw your birth.
May clouds ne'er lower their darksome mists around,
  May all thy life be like a summer day;
May loving friends on every side abound
  To help thee on when comes a rugged way;
May worldly cares be few and far between,
  May nought e'er dim this day of sweet delight;
May Heaven's tint gild o'er each earthly scene,
  And, when thy spirit fades into the night—
May guardian angels fly on wings of love
And carry it to brighter realms above.

IN THE TWILIGHT.

—

THOUGH old and worn, and furrowed by the hand
    That time lays on the heads of young and old;
I still am circled by that golden band
    And from my soul no gloom has to be rolled.
Sweet gleams of sunshine steal into my heart,
    And whisper to me words of love and peace,
Which to my breast a tenfold joy impart.
    That earthly cares can never make decrease.
No vain regrets disturb my even way—
    The past can only once in life be trod;
The present time is mine—the coming day
    With blest content I leave unto my God.
No shadows hover round my eventide,
For trust, and hope, doth e'er with me abide.

THE FLIGHT OF TIME.*

TIME writes his wrinkles on my haggard brow,
    And stamps old age with harmony of thought ;
Ah me! that to his dictates all must bow,
    And stand upon the brink with danger fraught.
In vain we long for days of old once more—
    In vain we sigh o'er visions of the past—
In vain our errors and neglects deplore—
    Time's retributive hand has come at last.
And, after all, age is a welcome boon —
    The golden rest of earnest duty done ;
We would not have an everlasting June,
    Nor bask beneath an everlasting sun.
All works for good—my human life lies back,
Regret is all that lines the beaten track.

---

* This Sonnet is the joint production of the Author and a Poetical Friend.
the lines being written alternately.

TO HER MAJESTY THE QUEEN OF ROUMANIA.*

—

DEAR Lady, at that blest and hallowed shrine,
   Which only Bards can ever hope to know,
I long have worshipped, and have felt the glow
Which sweetly clings about that fount divine.
The poet's realm, too, has for years been thine,
   It is a realm which ever seems to grow,
   And those who live there, to the world bestow
The buds and blossoms of the glorious Nine.

These are my buds—mayhap not ripened yet,
   But still I culled them in that wondrous land
   Where all is holy, beautiful and grand,
And trust they soon will richer bloom beget.

   Long may the Muse, dear Queen, her charms expand,
   Proving to thee a fairy amulet.

---

* Who, through her Secretary, requested a copy of the Author's Poems.

TO HENRY I. BUTTERFIELD, ESQ.,*

OF CLIFFE CASTLE, KEIGHLEY.

IN accents low I heard a poet sing,
　　Scorn not, oh man! the bard of humble worth;
　　His is the task to dignify the earth,
And with sweet song sooth sorrow's sordid sting
With many a lay of wild imagining.
　　The land that gave to Saxon Kihel birth,
　　Whate'er its faults and flaws, has had no dearth
Of those whose songs have made its valleys ring.

From many pens these gems of verse are brought,
　　Some rich in language where the glowing mind
　　Speaks out in eloquence; some unrefined—
But all at Poesy's blest shrine have wrought.

　　As tribute to thy native town and thee
　　I tend these children of Melpomene.

---

* This sonnet appeared as the dedication in one of the Author's works entitled "The Poets of Keighley, Bingley, and District."

DAY DREAMS.

—

PAST, present, future, these are pregnant themes
    Which fill the poet's mind the long day o'er;
These are to him his ever choice day-dreams,
    They hold for him, of wealth, a golden store.
Perchance he dreams of what he yet may be,
    Or else he dreams of what has long been his,
E'en tho' he dreams of hoar antiquity
    Each proves to him a very mine of bliss.
A lover now—a man grown old in years;
    A little child with never thought of woe—
All these before his wondering brain appears
    As things that are, or what he still may know.
They thrill with joy at will, or taunt with pain,
And yet he longs to dream them o'er again.

TO THE STARS.

—

Y̆E confuse coronets of celestial grace,
    That brightly gild the arching dome of Heaven;
Say, why ye float amid unending space,
    By circling whirlwinds furiously driven?
Or, brightly beaming through the crystal night
    Without the slightest motion, are at rest
Save for the twinklings of serenest light,
    With which ye have earth's creatures ever blest?
Lo! the Stars answer, "There shall come a day
    When all shall fathom things that now seem strange,
And nought so boundless but will show the way,
    Whate'er their vast immensity of range!
When, like the pages of an open book
All men may learn who pause awhile and look.

CHRISTMAS.

—

HAIL, Father Christmas! King of all the year,
   We welcome thee, all clad in vestments white,
   Thou bring'st to us the holly berries bright,
And shar'st with us thy kindly, gladd'ning cheer.
Would'st know why thou to us art ever dear?
   It is because thy coming bringeth light—
   Dispelling all the dull, dark caves of night,
Illuming them, till all the scene is clear.
Thou bring'st together those whom cruel time
   Has parted from a loving parents' breast;
   By thousands thou art honoured, loved and blest,
In every country and in every clime:
No wonder, then, that all thy praises sing.
And crown thee, Christmas, Earth's Majestic King.

AT THE STREAM.

I TROD, knee-deep, the soft, luxuriant grass,
  Until I came beside a sportive stream ;
Which seemed to sing, "Oh! do not by me pass,
  Till thou hast told me of thy pleasant dream."
For I was dreaming—a sweet, longing dream,
  Of endless summer and undying love ;
And I was so enchanted with the theme
  I heeded not the darkening clouds above.
Methought how sweet 'twould be—how passing sweet
  If life could be one bright, unending day ;
With sunlit streams and sylvan shades replete,
  And blooming blossoms on each verdant spray.
But 'mid my revellings in the swelling strain
My dream was banished by a shower of rain.

THE IDIOT.

THE light of reason from his eyes has fled,
    His form is bent, though youth is in its prime;
His shoulders scarce support his drooping head,
    A head unsullied by the taint of crime.
How pale and wan his sickly face appears—
    How long and thin—how coldly moist his hand;
No pleasures he—nor hopes, nor aims, nor fears,
    A vacant creature in a vacant land.
How spare his hair—how very sleek and lank;
    Deprived of thought from uneventful birth
All is to him one, long, continuous blank—
    One harsh, strong fetter, binding him to earth.
But soon the chain which holds his mind will break,
And, in the realm of boundless thought he'll wake.

A VISION.

I SAW a form devoid of plan or shape,
   Steal in my room one lonely, stormy night;
And there with many a grin grotesque and gape,
   It filled me with a feeling of affright.
My trembling lips refused a word utter—
   And then, this phantom—shadow, if you will
Leered o'er my body and commenced to mutter
   In harsh weird tones " You feeble one, be still;
I am the vision known as restlessness,
   I give no solace to the creature, man ;
Nor soothe him in his terror or distress
   But bind him firmly 'neath my powerful ban.
I give no peace nor comfort—but destroy
His present hopes and all his future joy."

AT AUDLEY.*

—

WITHOUT the lyre of Nature none can sing
    Except in feeble tones and puny strains;
And nature cannot be compelled to bring
    Her lyre to those who promise sordid gains,
And yet, when here, e'en had I not the soul
    Of sweet, refreshing, gentle poesy—
Methinks the echoes of her lyre would roll
    Their thrilling whispers even unto me;
And haunt me long, and leave me not till I
    Perforce should be compelled to break in rhyme,
And tinted by their blissful sovereignty
    I left my footprints on the Sands of Time.
Like him who rests beneath this hallowed sod
The poet, and the minister of God.

---

* Whatever poetic proclivities the author may possess are mainly the result of knowing that his great uncle, the Rev. Thomas Garratt, M.A. (many years Vicar of Audley), was a minor poet of the first rank, at the beginning of the present century, and author of numerous works of a poetical and theological character.

AT NEWCHAPEL.*

THE dear, old place is much the same to me
 As when a boy, with happy mind and gay,
I trod its lanes with joyous step and free,
 Thinking no future could my day-dreams slay.
But ah! though time will for a space forget
 To harshly deal with fabrics raised by man;
All human kind he grasps within his net,
 Nor always waits till they have reached life's span.
The forms and faces once to me so dear
 Have long since left this world of grief and woe;
And yet to-day I feel that they are near,
 Whispering to me with loving voice and low;
And bidding me to watch and hope and wait
For their sweet welcome at the Golden Gate.

---

* The author's grandfather, the Rev. Thurstan Forshaw (a St. Bees student, E. 1831), was for nearly thirty-five years the Vicar of Newchapel.

AN INCIDENT.*

METHINKS upon the calm sea-scented air
    The cry of " Fire," breaks the hush of night;
Methinks I see cheeks blanchéd by despair,
    And eager footsteps trembling with affright,
I fancy, too, that willing hands and strong
    From out the burning house bring all they can;
Debarred not by the flame's devouring tongue,
    But working well to help a fellow man,
I see the flames extinguished, and I see
    The little groups of students gathered near;
I hear their consolating sympathy,
    Saying that now. "there is no cause for fear."
And ah! I hear the thanks that *they* outpoured,
Thanks for their peril passed, thanks to the Lord.

---

* Amongst the many St. Bees' men who kindly ordered copies of this work prior to its publication, is the Rev. R. Parry Burnett, Vicar of Stanwell, near Staines; seeing by the College Calendar that the author's grandfather was at St. Bees at the same time (1832) that Mr. Burnett was, the author wrote to the latter gentleman asking him if he recollected his grandfather. The Rev. gentleman replied as follows: "I well remember your grandfather, and was pleased in having his acquaintance, his lodgings were not far from mine and I recollect a fire occurring in them one night, and his having to turn out in great haste with his things." The sonnet is founded on this event.

A SERMON.

A SABBATH eve—and all around was peace—
   A dear old Church, slow-crumbling to decay—
God's servant speaking words of hallowed grace,
   And pointing out the life, the truth, the way.
His voice so earnest thrilled my listening ear,
   'Minding me now of that calm summer's night
When, to his flock, he said in accents clear—
   'He was a burning and a shining light.'*
And bade his hearers to so live their days
   That, like St. John, they be prepared for heaven,
And, falling not in worldom's wicked ways,
   To hope, and trust, and pray to be forgiven;
So that when dead their light to all will shine
Showing they lived on earth for life divine.

---

* Whilst staying with the Rev. James Gabb, B.A. Rector of Bulmer, the author had the privilege of hearing the Rev. gentleman preach from this text, in the quaint old church at Bulmer, on June 21st, 1891,

TO W. SCRUTON.*

NO more the harsh despoilers of our land
　　Can revel in their wasteful, wanton crime,
　When they erase from dear old Bradford's clime
The ancient spots that once e'en they deemed grand!
For lo! with loving touch of master hand,
　　Old scenes are raised, and now in words sublime,
　　We tread the long extent of backward time;
For Scruton here, has well and wisely planned
Those pleasant ways which still we love so well;
　　And with painstaking but triumphant pen,
　　He makes us live the dear old days again
On which our memory doth so often dwell.
　　Once more our eyes take in each old time sight,
　　And give to us sweet visions of delight.

* Author of ,, Pen and Pencil Pictures of Old Bradford."

SMITH.

—

HAVING ten minutes I'd nought to do with,
    I sit my self down and poetical brood,
      And feeling, somehow, in poetical mood
I thought I would write a sonnet on Smith.
Smith's a fine fellow—of humour the pith,
    Graceful and gentle, and gallant and good,
      He never is vulgar, discourteous, or rude,
Albeit his surname is nowise a myth.
Smith is a gentleman, loving and true,
    Clever, kind-hearted, frank, fearless and free,
And if you'd to search the universe through,
      You'd not find a man more manly than he.
Yes! Smith is a MAN, *sans* sin and *sans* shame,
But look at the beggar's unfortunate name.

IN MEMORIAM.

CARDINAL NEWMAN.

" The Saint and Poet will in him survive."—'TIMES.'

LEAD kindly light.   Ah! light at last has led
   The poet through the portals of that shrine,
   Where all is holy, beautiful, divine.
How oft when here below his light he shed,
And all his flock with God-like wisdom fed ;
   Until his light from out its own confine
   Burst all its bonds to grow and intertwine
Amongst the dark, till all the gloom had fled.

Night now has gone ! no more amid the gloom,
   Wandereth the master mind—the brilliant pen ;
   The step is taken—now the prince of men
Has left his earthly for his heavenly home.
Immortal life! now freed from earthly gyve,
The Saint and Poet will indeed survive.

IN MEMORIAM.

THE REV. KNIGHT GALE, A.K.C.*

ONE lab'rer left the vineyard—nothing more;
 One worker home, his earthly toil now done,
 And well he has his crown of glory won
On Heaven's Elysian, bright and golden shore.
After the cross the crown.   Earth's days are o'er;
 Quickly they pass, and life's short race is run;
 But now in realms of everlasting sun
He lives for aye.   Why then his death deplore?

Let us be patient: there is One knows best;
 Let us repine not, neither let us weep;
 God's love for us is firm, and strong, and deep,
We've but to trust to join him 'mong the blest.
 Let us sow well—we then like him shall reap
The bounteous harvest of eternal rest.

---

* For nearly thirty-eight years the Vicar of St. Andrew's, Bradford.

IN MEMORIAM.

MRS. G.

—

GONE to her rest—the worn and weary soul,
  Gone to that realm, where from all care she's free,
  Where through the vastness of Eternity
She'll dwell with God, by His great love made whole.
Peace came at last, and now within that goal
  She lives a life of blest felicity,
  That life of love—that life of liberty
Which knows no end though countless seasons roll.
Mourn not, ye friends, her spirit is at peace;
  Mourn not, ye children—ye who loved her well,
Her time had come, and now no earthly lease
  Bindeth her body where the soul doth well!
But watch ye—pray ye—never, never cease,
  And ye shall join her in Heaven's citadel.

IN MEMORIAM

B.

NOT long his sojourn in this world of cares,
　　Not long his stay on this tempestuous earth,
God now has answered all his heartfelt prayers
　　And to him given an Eternal Birth.
He prayed the Lord to take his soul above,
　　To free it from its earthly bonds below;
From worldly thraldom to the Courts of Love
　　Is but a step—that step we all must know.
Let us not murmur then, at Time's decree,
　　For when our warfare on this earth is o'er,
Our souls to Heaven's Elysian Realms will flee,
　　And join our loved ones' on the golden shore.
Where happiness eternal shall endure
Where all is holy, good and bright and pure.

IN MEMORIAM.

H.

———

ONCE more with ruthless stroke stern death steps in,
    This time a sister sinks beneath his hand;
'Tis God's good plan, and here she well did win
    A crown of glory in the Better Land.
Long suffering she. and yet she murmured not,
    But meekly to the Voice Divine did bow;
And tho' on earth her's was a bitter lot,
    She dwells among the Holy Angels now.
Her's was a glorious death—the King of kings
    Gave her that peace which only He can give,
And now beneath the shadow of His wings,
    For ever and for ever she will live
In worlds where come not death, nor pain, nor sin,
Where but the righteous ones can enter in.

IN MEMORIAM.

L.

FORGIVE us, Lord, if now our grieved hearts cry
　　Against those words of sorrow, "dust to dust,"
For 'tis so hard to see the young ones die—
　　Help us, O Lord, and give us strength to trust.
We would not murmur, Lord, but we are weak,
　　And all Thou dost, Thou doest for the best;
Oh! teach us still on earth Thy praise to speak,
　　Thou but hast given Thy belovéd rest.
She is an early-folded lamb ; Thy home
　　Beyond the skies was for such loved ones given,
And Thy sweet voice said "Let the children come,
　　For of such is the Kingdom of Heaven."
Therefore, O Lord, we wait 'the little while'
When she will welcome us with loving smile.

TO ZEUS.*

—

GREAT god of wisdom! high my voice I raise,
    And speed to thee a lay deep from my heart,
A lay of admiration and of praise.

    None other ever was thy counterpart,
Nor yet shall be though ages flee away,
    New worlds arise, new planets come and go,
Thy fame's eternal—knowing no decay.

    No tarnish comes to take away the glow ;
Thou art the sire of the immortal fair—
    The glorious damsels of unfading youth,
Whose classic heads and brightly laurell'd hair
    Speak of Sincerity—allied with Truth.
This, noble Zeus, proclaims to one and all
That from thy pedestal, thou ne'er wilt fall.

---

*Zeus and Mnemosyne were the parents of the nine muses of the Greek mythology—Calliope, Clio, Melpomene, Thalia, Euterpe, Terpsichore, Erato, Polyhymnia, and Urania. Pieria in Macedonia was their first dwelling-place. Only three were originally worshipped in Helicon—Melete, Mneme and Aoide—or Reflection, Memory and Song. The peculiar attributes given to the sister goddesses by the Author are based on the powers originally assigned to them by the poets.

TO MNEMOSYNE.

GODDESS of memory! sweet Mnemosyne,
    Fill thou the chasms of my wandering brain;
Impart to me that gay exuberancy
    Which banisheth rebellious thoughts of pain.
Then shall my tongue as tho' unloosed by wine
    Break forth from out the bonds that held it fast,
    And, 'stead of dark oblivions of the past
Shall come melodious utterances divine.
Unwearied from the pastureland of joy
    Then shall my fingers string the mellow lyre,
And nought shall come to injure or destroy
    Its fluttering pinions, as, on wings of fire
Trembling with ecstasy it swiftly flies
To lands immortal where it never dies.

TO CALLIOPE.

GODDESS of Grace I pray impart to me
      That eloquence which none but thou hast got;
Come when I call thee, coy Calliope—
      Come to me from thy sacred sylvan grot;
So that my words may issue full and free
      In boundless buoyancy. serene and bright,
      Swift as the sunbeam's radiant, sparkling light
Unfettered as the restless, surging sea.
So that I sing in brave heroic measure,
      Triumphantly and gloriously sublime;
No dull despondency to mar my pleasure
      Nought but one long. continuous, swelling chime;
Vibrating with its majesty of motion
The highest heaven and the deepest ocean.

TO CLIO.

—

SWEET maid of glowing beauty, all my soul
   Clings like a tendril to thy stately form ;
E'en all the gods thy dignity extol—
   So, a poor mortal, it may well transform.
Thy heaving bosom with a stainless pride—
   Rises and falls in faultless symmetry ;
   As, breathing forth the loftiest purity
Thy lips, like corals, smilingly divide,
Issuing such notes of thrilling melody ;
   I scarce dare breathe for fear thy voice should cease
   But no! thy strains unfailingly increase
Giving such tinge of their blest harmony,
Enamouring me with such ecstatic joy —
I tremble lest earth's scenes should it destroy.

TO MELPOMENE.

MELPOMENE, thou tragedaic queen,
      No roseate hues bestrew thy way with flowers,
  No ambient tints enlight thy darksome hours—
Thou sing'st of nought jocundous or serene.
Thou but depicts a stern and sombre scene,
      Full of tempestuous wailings of despair
      Which hang around the dull and heavy air
Bedimming—like a storm-cloud—the terrene.
Thou sing'st of falseness, treachery, deceit,
      Of love's fair passion turned to hate and scorn,
      Nor giveth hope that on a brighter morn
Glad songs shall come to make thine obsolete.
And yet, Melpomene, thy power is grand—
Thy teaching's pregnant over all the land.

TO THALIA.

—

COME sweetest sprite, unlock the gates of joy,
　　And let me glide within thy fairy realm;
Or let me sail on streams that never cloy,
　　It matters not if thou art at the helm
To guide my thoughts like meteors bright and free,
　　Into the home of loveliness and smiles,
Where sin and shame and sorrow ne'er can be;
　　And where each scene the rapturous thought beguiles.
Where every breath is rich with fragrant sweets
　　Charged with the essence of ten thousand flowers,
And where the heart with gladness wildly beats
　　So Eden-like, so Heavenly are the bowers.
Where waves of melody come floating o'er,
Soft-echoing to me from thy golden shore.

TO EUTERPE.

—

THOU all sustaining ruler of the bard,
   Guide my numb hand and give it will and power
  To glide along.　'Freshed by thy dewy shower
Nought can its flowing suppleness retard.
'Neath thy bewitching thraldom I would bend,
  So that my song can issue freely forth
Knowing no boundary, delay or end
  Throughout the wide expanse of all the earth.
Prolong my verse to music silvery,
  Weed all its feebleness, and cast aside
  All that thou would'st not have with thee abide,
All but the purest of my minstrelsy ;
So that though weak, I still have strength to stray
Along the groves of each Parnassian way.

TO TERPSICHORE.

—

YE earthly sounds be silent! Let my ear
　　Bask in the melting music of thy strains—
Strains which come not to this terrestrial sphere,
　　But are eternal on thy heavenly plains.
Thy voice is wedded to the sacred lyre
　　Thy nimble fingers touch with such sweet might,
With power achillic that can never tire
　　Nor ever fail to give supreme delight.
Now wavering like a gentle zephyr breeze—
　　Now trembling like the wavelets on the shore,—
Now like the thunderings of the storm-tossed seas—
　　Making the mighty cringe beneath its roar,
Then, light and gentle as the bulbul's notes
It softly dies, and silent from us floats.

TO ERATO.

—

DESCEND Erato, with thy living fire,
　　And flood my mind with thine enchanting strains;
Let me a moment all thy power inspire:
　　Fill my rapt bosom with ecstatic rains !
Erato comes, but whispers in mine ear
　　"Only one moment shalt thou have mine aid,"
So I, perforce, whilst yet she lingereth near
　　Bask in the radiant atmosphere she made,
And as I breathe, sweet incense o'er me steals—
　　I feel intoxicated as with wine ;
My pulses throb, my poor brain wildly reels
　　With deepest rapture at the joy divine.
Ah me ! if bliss—o'erpowering bliss, could kill
I'd sure been slain, so great was kind Erato's thrill.

TO POLYHYMNIA.

—

THOU "many-hymned-one," thou who first did form
    The soft and tuneful, soul-enchanting lyre ;
I hear thy melody above the storm
    For thou it is our lyric songs inspire.
Silently sitting in a studious mood
    A graceful poise about thy classic head ;
Thy eyes denote sublime beatitude—
    Thy face bespeaks of thoughtfulness inbred.
And, as thou riseth with thy lyre in hand
    Something bewitches me, as if a potion
Sent me a glimpse of fairest fairyland.
    Then know I 'tis the poetry of motion
Fresh from the region of Parnassian dews,
And which thou send'st to those who woo the muse.

TO URANIA.

—

BLEST maid of purest attributes divine—
 Of god-like wisdom and celestial grace;
Thou art the chief of all the Sisters Nine
 For heaven itself's reflected in thy face.
Seraphic being! How shall I give praise
 To thee whose tones nigh silence angels' tongues?
To thee—whose fervent, rich and full-voiced lays
 Surpass in majesty their sweetest songs?
Thrice blessed Urania! Nay ten thousand times
 Art thou thrice blest, for thou canst sway all hearts
Both here, on earth, and in eternal climes,
 And still thy song flows on. and still imparts
To mortals here, to cherubim above
The mighty influence of surpassing love.

TO MELETE.

—

ⁿO haste unseemly, lovely Melete
　　Dost thou permit with those who seek thine aid;
And, when thy lover's come to worship thee—
　　If thou in Helicon should'st be delayed;
Thou dost not go to them with vulgar speed—
　　But thinkest thrice what it were best to do.
And none can blame thee for this perfect creed;
　　Thy satellites come hurriedly to woo
Without that quality—consideration;
　　So that they overstep Queen Wisdom's bound,
And find, too late, it was imagination
　　That plunged them on a dark and treacherous ground.
But, led by thee—thou goddess of delight,
All things show plainly, e'en to mortal sight.

TO MNEME.

—

WITHOUT thy aid blest Mneme, man would be
　　Less than the brute, an aimless, senseless thing,
Inanimate, and void of energy—
　　A poor, frail clod, past all recovering.
But charmed by thee, and given recollection,
　　He is the king and ruler of the world,
And thy great gift with Melete's reflection
　　Shall cause his banner to remain unfurled,
While the earth lasts, while day and night appears,
　　While seasons come and go ; so long sweet maid
　　Shall mortals seek the glamour of thy shade—
And dwell in it through all the coming years.
For thou instilleth them with new surprise
And daily maketh them more pure and wise.

TO AOIDE.

—

TRIUMPHANT Empress of all tuneful song—
   Spirit of lavish gaiety supreme—
Bounding and leaping joyously along,
   Thy flowing numbers are a sunlit gleam
To light our path to heaven-born joys above;
   Glimmering incessantly, they sparkling shine,
And speak of chaste and sempiternal love—
   Which worlds of darkness cannot undermine.
Bright as a rivulet of molten gold
   Swift as the lightning—gorgeous as the sun
   Thy strains flow on, and softly sighing, run
Into some dazzling ocean, brave and bold.
Nought can compare, oh! peerless Aoide
With the bright beacons of thy harmony.

TO LETHE.*

—

OH! Lethe, of thy draught, forgetfulness
　　I fain would drink, and drinking steep my brain
In that oblivion which soothes distress
　　And banishes the former pangs of pain.
The past I would erase from off the scroll
　　Of my existence—I would obliterate
The sins I have committed, and my soul
　　Would then be purged and lightened, and the weight
Which weighs it down, would fall, and I should be
Blithe as the bird, for should I not be free
　　Of this absorbing, overwhelming woe,
That hurls me into gulphs of dark despair,
Where all is dismal with depressent care,
　　So full of Stygian horrors is its flow?

---

* In Greek mythology, Lethe is the river of oblivion. Its water possessed the quality of causing those who drank it to forget the whole of their former existence.

NIOBE *

OH! stern Apollo! oh! cruel Artemis!
    To slay the offspring of good Niobe ;
Is it not every mother's constant bliss
    To aye extol the babe upon her knee ?
Sure every mother's loved one is the best,
    And charms possess, and beauty and delight,
And grace, which far surpasseth all the rest—
    And are to them perfection's sacred height.
Poor Niobe was only like to them ;
    Her nurselings were the kings and queens of earth,
    Rare jewels in her crown—of priceless worth—
Each was to her a sparkling diadem.
No wonder that amid her bitter moan,
The gods in their compassion made Niobe stone.

---

* Niobe was the wife of Amphion, king of Thebes. By extolling the superior beauty of
her six sons and six daughters, she incurred the wrath of Apollo and Artemis, who slew them,
Niobe's grief changed her into stone.

TO ETA.

—

HADST thou, sweet maiden, lived in ancient days
    Methinks each daughter of Mnemosyne
Would envy thee thy brightly-laurelled bays,
    Which crown thee queen of truth and purity.
High Jove has planted in thy pregnant brain
    The seeds he sows with such a careful hand ;
    The shoots have risen, and the flowerets grand
Wave here and there—making the barren plain
Into a lovely Eden—for his rain
    Has nurtured them, and soon o'er all the land
    The blossoms he so beautifully planned
Will shed their odours, which will long remain.
Sing on, blest Eta, there shall come a day
When all the world is better for thy sway.

LYRICS.

THE STREAMLET.*

SEE the sparkling streamlet
   Babbling on its way,
Over moss and pebbles
   How it loves to stray ;
Running thro' the meadows,
   Glancing in the suu ;
Thro' the meads and pastures
   See it blithely run.

---

* Music by Mr. A. W. Whitaker, of Bradford.

See the sparkling streamlet,
   Watch it onward glide ;
Ever bright and sportive
   Seeming full of pride.
Rippling, singing gaily,
   Full of mirth and glee,
Home to Mother River,
   Home to Father Sea.

See the sparkling streamlet
   Roaming thro' the dell,
Thro' the glade and forest,
   Thro' the wood and fell.
List its gentle murmur,
   Watch its prank and play ;
Never, never tiring,
   Careless as the day.

See the sparkling streamlet
  Romping, bubbling past,
Onward to the ocean
  Flows it now at last.
Dashing, splashing, madly,
  Hark its mighty roar;
Surging, whelming strongly,
  'Tis a stream no more.

CHRISTMAS.

—

SEASON of mistletoe, season of holly,
Season of happiness, season of glee;
Season of gaiety, joyous and jolly
Season of jests which at yule-tide run free.

Season of merriment, season of teasing,
Season of almonds and raisins and wine;
Season of dancing, and kissing, and squeezing,
Season when everyone ' kicks up a shine.'

Season of frostiness, season of ' rinking,'
Season of turkey and rabbit and goose;
Season of puddings and mincepie and ' drinking ';
Season of headaches for those ' on the loose.'

Season of carolling, season of giving,
Season of music, of mirth and of light,
Season which tells us that ' life IS worth living,'
Season when bed does'nt claim us at night.

Season of puzzles, charading and singing,
Season of pantomime, season of cheer ;
Season that proveth old time e'er is winging,
Season that bringeth the close of the year.

DRIFTING.

—

OUT on the billowy ocean
    Hitherward, thitherward, driven,
With never a soothing potion
    For my heart so anguish-riven.
Nothing but waste of waters—
    For my longing eyes to see,
Nothing but miles of billows,
    Nought but the trackless sea,—
And nothing to comfort, cheer or bless
My lonesome heart in its loneliness.

Lashed to a piece of timber,
　At the mercy of the wind;
Where can I look for a haven,
　And where shall I harbour find?
The fathomless waves give answer
　Deep down in the depths below
Are the graves of many a mortal—
　And there thou too must go.
And the foaming waves of the treacherous sea
Seem to laugh aloud in their fiendish glee.

SHE'LL BE COMING BY AND BYE.

QUICKLY pass ye tardy moments
   Send to me the blissful hours
When once more I am with Kitty
   Roaming through the roseate bowers,
Time, alas! went ne'er so slowly,
   Haste ye laggards, swiftly fly ;
And time whispers, patience, patience,
   She'll be coming by and bye.

Still I wait, but Kitty lingers—
   Careless sprite where can she be
Yet full well she knows I'm waiting,
   Waiting by the trysting tree.
Lazy moments, why so straggling ?
   Do for once please faster fly,
But they echo, patience, patience,
   She'll be coming by and bye.

Hark! I hear her dainty footsteps—
   Sweetest music to my ear,
And my arms will soon enfold her,
   For sweet Kitty cometh near.
Stay ye moments! why so rapid ?
   Why so quickly onward fly ?
They retort but ne'er so archly
   She'll be GOING by and bye.

SONG.

—

WHEN some wave of wild emotion
 Fills the breast with sweetest glee—
Such as rippling of the ocean
 Dancing in its buoyancy.
Then my heart is filled with gladness.
 And my bosom leaps with joy,
And no thought of future sadness,
 Comes my day-dreams to destroy.

Or beside some gentle river
 Flowing onward to the sea—
Singing sweet, I run for ever,
 What so gay and blithe as me?
Then my soul all sorrow spurning
 Sings a song of sweetest joy,
And no thought of grief returning.
 Comes my day-dreams to destroy.

If I stray in Summer meadows
  Gathering flowers gay and bright,
Comes no thought of hov'ring shadows
  To repel my long delight.
Nothing but ten thousand blisses
  Speak to me of present joy,
And no thought of time's remisses
  Comes my day-dreams to destroy.

YULE TIDE.

—

THRICE welcome, Father Christmas,
   A pleasant guest art thou,
With stately form and hoary,
   With brightly laurell'd brow;
Thou com'st to cheer the careworn
   For thine's a gladsome heart;
To many a lonely bosom
   Thou dost true joy impart.

At this our festive season,
   We hail thee as our king;
For friends that time has parted
   Together thou dost bring.
And many a gentle mother,
   And many a stern old sire,
Heap on thee richest blessings
   When round thy glowing fire,

And e'en the little children
　Are filled with mirth and glee,
With rippling peals of laughter—
　When they thy coming see;
For well they know thou bringest
　To each of them good cheer;
No wonder, then, they hail thee
　The king of all the year.

ANNIE BROWN.

MY heart is laid in an old churchyard
  For my love lies buried there;
My love I loved with my manhood's love—
 My love with the golden hair.
And the green, green grass above her waves,
 And the smiling sun looks down.
And the grey, old church seems keeping watch
 O'er my lovely Annie Brown.
But my heart is lone, and sad, and cold—
For deep it lies 'neath the churchyard mould.

Ah me! that the tyrant Death should reign
 With such firm and regal sway ;
Alas ! that he stole the love of my heart
 My love for ever and aye ;
And gaily the birds sing overhead,
 The bustling goes on in the town,
And the world has ne'er a thought to spare
 For my lovely Annie Brown.
But my heart is lone, and sad, and cold,
For deep it lies 'neath the churchyard mould.

HAPPY CHRISTMAS BELLS.*

—

RING out the gladsome tidings
    Ye bells from far and near—
Pour forth the thrilling chorus,
    Throughout each hemisphere ;
In accents clear and joyous
    Let every sound be heard,
The true, heartfelt thanksgiving
    That struggles into word.

And now ye hills, re-echo
    Those joyous strains afar ;
To ocean's deepest crevice—
    To Heaven's brightest star ;
Till with a sound triumphant—
    Through wood, and dale, and dells,
We hear the glorious murmur
    Of happy Christmas Bells.

---

* Music by the late eminent professer, Sydney Smith,—the last piece ever composed by
him.   The words are slightly altered from the Author's poem "The Year of Jubilee" which
are under the direct patronage of Her Majesty.

Now, glow ye youthful faces,
　　And beat, ye swelling hearts ;
With rapture, still increasing
　　Each nerve and heartstring starts ;
Ye bosoms ever tender
　　Are still more tender now ;
Your eyes with brightness sparkle,
　　And gladness beams on brow.

So now, ye youths and maidens,
　　Uplift the tuneful voice—
With cadence soft and lowly
　　And bid the world rejoice.—
Now, gratitude o'erwhelms us
　　With joy each glad heart wells
For, lo! we hear the music
　　Of happy Christmas Bells.

The old, old joyous story,
  With sunshine fills the soul ;
This ever welcome tidings
  Stretches from pole to pole ;
So lift once more your voices
  Bid care and discord cease,
And live and love in unity,
  In joy and hope and peace.

We raise our hearts to Heaven,
  And thank the God above,
For this most bounteous blessing
  That tells but of His love ;
And now with hope in Jesus
  Each bosom wildly swells ;
Hark now! that sound of mercy—
  The happy Christmas Bells.

NELL.

I ROAMED with artful Cupid
   Adown a flowery dell—
But Cupid was my darling,
   My bonny, bright-eyed Nell.

Her hair in wavy ringlets
   Upon her shoulders fell,
And I caressed the tresses,
   And called her pretty Nell.

And in her ear I whispered
   The words we love so well,
The old but new love-story,
   To graceful, queenly Nell.

I saw her drooping eyelids
  Spoke more than words could tell;
Then knew I that she loved me—
  My own bewitching Nell.

And soon in yonder cottage
  My love and I shall dwell;
My love, my own for ever,
  My little sweetheart, Nell.

RONDEAUX.

SWEET MOTHER, DEAR.

SWEET mother, dear, though storm-clouds lower
  And make your heart full sad and sore,
  Dark'ning this erstwhile gladsome day,
  Making you feel that "life's rough way"
Has only countless griefs in store.

Remember, He on yonder shore
All your long troubles watches o'er ;
  Your sorrows will not last for aye
                Sweet mother dear.

Oh! do not then to-day deplore,
As time flies on I'll love you more ;
  I'll be your hope, your friend, your stay,
  And ever for you, dear, will pray,
As oft I've fervent prayed before
                Sweet mother dear.

WHILST WITH MY BOOKS.

—

WHILST with my books no cares have I
    To bring the teardrop to my eye;
And nought to mar the happiness
That oft has soothed me in distress
And bade my woes to quickly fly.

Thus I can all my griefs defy,
And to my troubles say " Good-bye,"
    And think on all with tenderness,
        Whilst with my books.

No outward throb, no inward sigh,
Has ever yet to me come nigh;
    No feeling fraught with loneliness,
    No harboured wrong to want redress,
All things but gladness, dormant lie
        Whilst with my books.

IT   MATTERS   NOT.

—

IT matters not, the lovers said—
We are determined to be wed,
And years to come will only prove
The depths of our undying love—
A love that has not thought of dread.

By artful Cupid fondly led,
And by his manna ever fed,
They still sing on where'er they rove—
It matters not.

No shadows would be overspread,
And woes—if any—soon be fled
If, trusting in the One above,
We daily struggled to improve,
And still could say—where'er we tread—
It matters not.

'TIS GOOD TO STROLL.

'TIS good to stroll by leafy ways,
　　In Spring-time's mellow, later days;
　When bush, and tree, and knoll, are drest
　In Nature's shiny, verdant vest—
When each field has an emerald's blaze.

When, listening to the songster's lays
The mother bird her home pourtrays;
　　We think, when gazing on the nest—
　　　　　　　'Tis good to stroll.

And list their joyful song of praise,
With which they all the woodland's raise
　　When first they learn our quiet quest
　　Has not disturbed their darlings' rest:
To see such things of joy, displays
　　　　　　　'Tis good to stroll.

IN FALLOW FIELDS.

—

IN fallow fields I love to lie
  And watch the fleecy clouds on high;
Or, on the banks of limpid stream
To ponder listlessly, and dream
Of sun, and moon, and stars, and sky.

'Tis then the time slips swiftly by;
'Tis then the earth we deify;
  'Tis then we feel a joy supreme—
          In fallow fields.

'Tis there you anger modify;
'Tis there you nature fortify;
  'Tis there you catch a transient beam
  Of that far-off eternal gleam
Which all the world does dignify—
          In fallow fields.

SHE LITTLE KNOWS.

—

SHE little knows how my fond heart
   Is mutilated by her dart;
  She little thinks my throbbing brain
  Seems well nigh bursting by the pain
Her cruel language did impart.

She guesses not the tear-drops start,
And recks she little of the smart,
   Which long my bosom has o'erlain—
       She little knows.

I daily tread the world's vast mart—
I daily see man's wile and art —
   And mix with those who strive for gain;
   But still no ease can I obtain—
No peace, no hope, now we're apart—
       She little knows.

I LOVED HER NOT.

—

I LOVED her not--so do not fret—
She always was a vain coquette—
　And full of artifice and pride;
　She always did her swains misguide
And round them wove her tangling net.

Her meshes never me beset;
I know no pang of harsh regret,
　She never can at me deride —
　　　　　I loved her not.

It is no trouble to forget!
Why should I wish we ne'er had met?
　I never lingered by her side
　To try and win her for my bride;
I never sought her worldly 'set'!
　　　　　I loved her not.

IN YOUTHFUL DAYS.

IN youthful days when all was gay
　How gladly passed the time away ;
　　From early morn to late at night
　　Was one long hour of pure delight—
Delight but known in childish play.

Along the lanes we loved to stray
With ne'er a thought for life's hard fray ;
　　All things were pleasant to the sight
　　　　In youthful days.

Ah! well I list we loved to stray
And toss the fragrant new-mown hay ;
　　Why should we think of future blight ?
　　The present time to us was bright ;
We never sang a doleful lay
　　　　In youthful days.

WHAT TIME WE WASTE.

—

WHAT time we waste in idle thought—
Time which once sold is ne'er rebought;
Time full of past or present pain ;
Time which, alas! we ne'er regain—
With curses or with blessings fraught.

Our earthly days are all too short ;
Much good, however, might be wrought
If men would heed the maxim plain—
What time we waste.

Time once escaped can ne'er be caught—
The good the fleeting moments brought
Is hurt and tarnished by the stain
That memory leaves upon the brain ;
So heed the lesson age has taught—
What time we waste.

COME, GENTLE MUSE.

—

COME, gentle muse, and dwell with me,
   And let me share thy pleasantry;
  The night thou turnest into day
  And grievous thoughts thou send'st away
Thou art a fay of fun and glee.

I care not if we sail the sea
Or stay on land—for whilst with thee
   I could not sing a sadsome lay,
         Come, gentle muse.

Though fastly bound, I should be free—
For thou detestest tyranny;
   And though I sink beneath thy sway
   I know 'tis but thy sprightly play;
Ah! thou canst ever witching be—
         Come, gentle muse.

FAR, FAR AWAY.

—

FAR, far away—too far to tell,
　　I wandered to a quiet dell;
And there beside a rugged stream
I had a sweet and tender dream—
A dream that seemed a subtle spell.

Methought that elfins here did dwell,
And this, their rustic citadel,
　　Was haunt of many a Poet's theme,
　　　　　　Far, far away.

Each fairy had a tiny cell
Made from the fragment of a shell,
　　And lighted by the glowing gleam
　　Of many a fire-fly's lustrous beam!
Ah me! that dreams one's thoughts expel
　　　　　　Far, far away.

IN SHIPLEY GLEN.

IN Shipley Glen, one afternoon
In radiant, sunny, leafy June—
   When all was fresh and bright and gay
   I went to wile the hours away;
And, ah! they flitted all too soon.

The songsters long had ceased their tune,
And to their little homes had gone;
   Yet I missed not their merry lay
           In Shipley Glen.

For Nature here has lavish thrown
Her gems—so I was not alone;
   I saw the rippling streamlet play
   All sparkling 'neath the sun's glad ray;
To townsmen 'tis a lavish boon—
           In Shipley Glen.

* A popular holiday resort near Bradford.

WHEN LIFE WAS YOUNG.

WHEN life was young, long years ago,
  All Nature wore a happy glow;
  Far cooler seemed the Summer breeze;
  Far greener seemed the leafy trees;
Alas! that we should older grow.

Time brings a weight of grief and woe
To all who wander here below;
  But woe and grief were mysteries
    When life was young.

When age comes on, 'tis then we know
The force of many a bitter blow;
  We long for days of youthful ease—
  For age is crabbed and hard to please;
We did not think it would be so
    When life was young.

OH! NOBLE DUKE.*

OH, noble Duke of Devonshire,
To those who twang the Poet's lyre
Thou'st ever proved a friend in need,
And well assistest to succeed
Those whom to poetry aspire.
Too oft the true poetic fire
Has been allowed to droop—expire—
By many who should intercede—
Oh! noble Duke.

But thou dost comfort e'er inspire,
And aids the bardling to acquire
The one thing needful in his creed,
Which provest thou a friend indeed;
Thou helpest on their keen desire,
Oh! noble Duke.

---

* His Grace of Devonshire is an encourager and supporter of Literature. The Author is deeply indebted to him for his repeated munificent patronage.

HE SHOOK MY HAND.*

—

HE shook my hand!—the mighty Shah
So I am now particular
  To whom I tend my British fist ;
  For I am Royal now I wist,
As much as though his scimitar
Had done it right and regular.
Yes, I am now a " Persian Star."
  So all you common mortals, list!
        He shook my hand.

Perhaps I am not on a par
With all his nobles titular ;
  But I can tell the satirist
  And every would-be humorist
That NASR-ET-DIN "the popular"
        He shook my hand.

* When the Shah of Persia was in England two years ago, the Author had the honour of shaking hands with His Majesty.

HE USED TO PREACH.*

—

HE used to preach in days gone by
  Of Him who dwells beyond the sky;
  He taught them to be true and just,
  To hope, to pray, to love, to trust,
And live for those blest realms on high.
But now he in the grave doth lie,
Waiting the day of destiny.
    That we, God's children were but dust—
          He used to preach.

Then let us with solemnity,
Simplicity, sincerity,—
    With mind and heart for heaven robust
    Our worldly wickedness adjust.
To live for immortality—
          He used to preach.

---

* A tribute to the memory of the Author's cousin, the Rev. Chas. J. Forshaw, M.A. who
for thirty years was Rector of Cricket Malherbie and twenty-nine years Vicar of Cudworth.

IN ALTCAR CHURCH.*

IN Altcar Church his voice was heard,
Speaking of God's most glorious word;
  And telling in that hallowed place
  Of Jesu and His boundless grace,
Of pardon sweet to those who erred,
And mercy giv'n by Christ the Lord.
He said "praise Him with one accord"
              In Altcar Church.

We all must cross that dreaded ford,
And our deeds here on earth record;
  Then let us now the truth embrace,
  And sin and worldliness efface,
And be like him who ministered—
              In Altcar Church.

---

* The Author's great uncle, the Rev. Chas. F. Forshaw, B.A. was head master of Ormskirk Grammar School, and for many years Rector of Altcar.

I'LL NE'ER REPINE.

I'LL ne'er repine at daily woes,
  For I can find a sweet repose
    From vanity of worldly things.
      And troublous thought of earthly stings,
In realms which none but poet knows.

I heed me not the critics blows,
Nor care for harsh words from my foes,
    As each day to me new joy brings
            I'll ne'er repine.

The realm of fairest fancy flows
Around me—and when I disclose
    To others my imaginings—
      The time flies on with lightning wings;
So whilst each day so pleasant goes—
            I'll ne'er repine.

WHILST LIFE SHALL LAST.

—

WHILST life shall last my love is thine,
    Oh tender rosebud—Gwendoline;
    Though days may come and years may fly
    My love is thine until I die
Thou dainty little gem of mine.

Nought can its trueness undermine,
Its depths thou never canst divine,
    To thee I'll never cause a sigh
                Whilst life shall last.

Ah! by thine eyes which lustrous shine—
Thou givest me the welcome sign;
    Which says "I'll love thee constantly
    Surpassing well, and ardently,"
And thou. my love, shalt ne'er repine
                Whilst life shall last.

LET OTHERS SING.

——

LET others sing in praise of wine
　　And call it cheering and divine,
　It never can to me impart
　The fierceness of its fiery dart,
Nor yet enchant me by its shine.

I have no Bacchanalian shrine
Nor crave to sip the juicy vine ;
　Of its ambrosial counterpart—
　　　　　　Let others sing.

Nor shall I e'er for it repine—
But to partake of it decline;
　Its burning lustre and its smart
　Shall never enter in my heart;
And if some think it superfine—
　　　　　　Let others sing.

MISCELLANEOUS POEMS.

LINES

WRITTEN IN THE ALBUM OF A LADY LIBRARIAN.

—

I WISH thee well—can I say more?
No, not if all the learnéd lore
Were mine which thou presidest o'er.

I wish thee well, may goodly store
Of blessings from the Heavenly shore,
Be thine for aye and evermore.

I wish thee well, and on life's way
May friends be with thee day by day
Making thy life an endless May.

I wish thee well—this tribute pay
And ask thee still to watch and pray
For strength to battle through life's fray.

VILLANELLE.

'TIS useless trying again
    I know I shall ne'er succeed,
My efforts are all in vain.

I have tried with might and main,
    Yet all things my aim impede,
'Tis useless trying again.

The thoughts of it give me pain.
    Though failure is not my creed,
My efforts are all in vain.

I have put forth ev'ry strain,
    I have striv'n with ev'ry plead,
'Tis useless trying again.

Yes, it goes against the grain,
    But I cannot make her heed,
My efforts are all in vain.

You may call me a laggard swain
    This advice I do not need,
'Tis useless trying again
    My efforts are all in vain.

FOR   AN   ALBUM.

—

THE Poet of all time, with Wisdom's voice,
  And clarion tones, said "all the world's a stage!"
Methinks far-seeing Shakespeare was not wrong
And though my pen grows feeble when I write
Th' immortal bard's renowned and noble name,
I'll use to-day another synonym.
The world I liken to a portrait book.
For lo! within its pages we can see
The prattling infant full of joy and mirth;
The child who never yet has known a care,
The youth and maiden in the flush of health
With nought to mar their present happiness.
The young man, full of hope—just ent'ring life,
And mayhap with him is his blooming bride,
Then we shall see his children on his knee,
And earthly cares begin, alas! to show

And leave their traces on his wrinkling cheek,
The years fly on, bringing a myriad cares,
Whit'ning the hair and furrowing the brow,
Bending the form which erstwhile was so straight.
And the companion of his joys and cares
Is harshly dealt with too—for Father Time
Respects no person in his flight through years.
But still we turn our album's pages o'er,
And now we look upon the well-known face
Of some dear friend who long ago has left
This tearful world for brighter realms above.
'Tis sad to miss the forms we loved so well—
To no more hear each well-remembered voice,
And bitter 'tis to miss the hand-clasp warm
Of one who many a time has greeted us.
But sweet it is to think in days to come,
We too shall join them in their home of bliss,
Where heartaches linger not, where youth prevails,
And where through countless ages we shall dwell
In untold glory, happiness and peace.

LEA.*

A DAZZLING vision burst upon my sight,
    And filled my being with untold delight ;
A lovely vision of angelic grace—
With pureness stamped on her bewitching face ;
With limbs like melting music, chaste, supreme,
An ever-present and enchanting dream.

How realistic to my wond'ring mind—
Past scenes, past pleasures, are left far behind ;
For in the vortex of my ecstacy
My soul's absorbed, nor longs it to be free.
Her stately splendour, so superb, so great,
Did all my senses seem to fascinate.

And oh! the liquid brightness of her eyes,
So full of radiant lustre and surprise.
In their sweet depths so mellow and divine,
The lamp of life does surely sparkling shine ;
So soft, so tender their expressive gaze,
Kind Heaven itself is centred in their rays.

---

* A Painting by Mr. J. E. Preston, of Littlebeck Hall, Gilstead.

Hush! do not wake me, let me still behold
The classic head, the hair of burnished gold;
Let me still gaze and see her standing there
Startled, surprised, but oh! surpassing fair.
Let my rapt eyes be filled with lasting bliss,
By gazing ever on a scene like this.

But do I dream? ah, no! yet still I see
The form—the face—so full of purity;
A goddess standing upon earthly land,
Formed by the pencil of a master-hand,
A form more fitted to the realms above,
A form to worship—to adore—to love.

Oh rare magician, who with paint can show
A human form that seems with life aglow,
Thy skill is heav'n-born in its wondrous sway,
Else scenes like this thou never could'st portray,
Oh may'st thou long thy worldly time employ
Creating creatures of celestial joy.

FAREWELL TO MORECAMBE.

—

FAREWELL till next year, oh! thou beautiful
    Morecambe,
Farewell to the scenes which I've learnt to love well;
Farewell to thy glories, so gaysome and joyous,
To all thy bright visions—a tender farewell.

When far from thy shores thy sweet beauties will
    haunt me,
And oft-times my bosom with gladness will fill,
Tho' other bright fancies sometimes will steal o'er me,
They cannot such raptures and joy-gleams instil.

I gaze on thy waters, they seem to bewitch me,
For gaily upon them fair Sol loves to shine,
No wonder that now when 'tis time I must leave thee
My heart's former gladness no longer is mine.

Sometimes when the winds lashed thy waves into
    fury,
Or if storm-fiends arose and drove them nigh mad ;
Or when scarce a ripple was seen on their surface,
Their changeable moods but made me the more glad.

And oft as I strolled on the rocks at dear Heysham,
To gaze on thy water's broad expanse below,
My soul throbbed with hope and with longing and
    yearning,
To stay in the place which my heart loveth so.

Farewell ! oh, farewell, all thy scenes are endearing,
No longer I gaze on the blue hills of Grange,
For now I return to town life's troublous story,
No wonder my heart grieveth sore at the change.

Farewell once again, the deep sorrow within me,
Welleth o'er and descends down my cheek in a tear,
Farewell, oh, farewell, there's one thought giveth
    comfort,
That thought—I shall see thee again in a year.

Morecambe, July 30th, 1890.

A PRESCRIPTION.

I CANNOT take the part of a Physician,
    Nor legally can I for the sick prescribe ;
But yet for once I shall make it my mission,
    And write a Prescription for the human tribe ;
The drugs I order are rich, rare and pure ;
Their properties for ever shall endure.

Take Sympathy and Kindness, mix them well,
Then triturate together. Warmth of Heart,
Friendship, Forgiveness and Benevolence,
Now add some Essence of Eternal Love—
The Tincture of Sweet Purity and Hope,
Mingling with these the Herbs of Joy and Trust.

These make a goodly mixture, still we're short

Of spices from Elysian Realms afar;
So now we take three parts of Honesty,
The same of Piety, Justice and Content.
Place these into the Bottle of your Heart,
Fill up with Wisdom and Sincerity,
And lest they should escape—seal well the cork.
I'll write the label: that we must affix,
My Medicine otherwise is incomplete.

To all mankind at this time of the year
    Extend these gifts so rich in Truth and Grace,
True Happiness to you will then appear,
    And Earth like Heaven will seem a Hallowed Place
Goodwill to Men will never, never cease,
Each heart will feel that blessing—Perfect Peace.

A REVERIE.

IN days gone by, when life was young,
  What chances passed away:
What pleasant visions o'er us hung
  Each livelong, happy day;
But they are gone beyond recall.
And live we now in worldom's thrall.

The old look back on childhood's days
  With mingled glee and sigh,
For all their ways were joyful ways,
  And youthful hopes ran high:
They wish for those blest days again—
Tho' wishing only gives them pain.

When they were young—'tis now the same—
  They longed for manhood's hours,
And tired, too soon, of boyish game
  Amid the fields and flowers.
Tho' now when age comes hast'ning fast
They long for days which long have past.

GUY FAWKES DAY.

NOW sounds of revelry and glee
    In many a town are heard;
And gladsome shouts of jollity
    And many a merry word
And squib and cracker loudly roar,
And sparks from bonfires upward soar.

But far from home, I musing sit,
    And think of days when I
Could join in this glad sport and wit
    With never care or sigh.
Ah! those were days when thoughts of woe
Would gently come and lightly go.

And here "far from the madding crowd"
    No cheerful blaze is seen;
And I hear not the cannon loud,
    Nor see the thrilling scene.
So my weak heart rebels in vain
That I can ne'er be young again.

Smalley, November 5th, 1891.

TO THE PRINCE OF WALES.*

—

THANKS, Royal Sir, for thy kind offering,
  It is a tribute that I long shall prize—
Thy thanks I value more because unsought.
A loyal heart within my bosom beats
And I am thankful that my feeble pen
Has given thee that pleasure, now expressed
In the kind note you cause to me be sent.
I am content to loiter at the foot
Of the Parnassian mountain—for I there—
In that blest valley of triumphant gods
Can breathe the air that other poets breathe,

And feel the mystic spells steal over me
That other Bards in other days have felt.
Yes! I am well content—so do not grieve
That my poor influence is less than theirs,
And in the coming up-hill fight for fame
Thy words will cheer, sustain and comfort me,
Proving to me an ever present help.

Spontaneous tokens of thy pleasure
To minstrels of such lowly worth as I
Are few and far between.   A royal prince
Has power to move the hearts of myriads;
And I shall be the better for thy words
So kindly and so generously sent.
Thy Silver Wedding moved a hundred bards
To tell the thankfulness their hearts evinced;
And though the least of all these many tongues,
I did not see a reason to refrain
To let my lyre—though humble—try to sing
A song to my illustrious, future King.

GLOZE.

NO hope is left for me,
I can no more be free!

All things seem dark and drear
And full of misery,
And tho' I know no fear
No hope is left for me!

My thoughts are full of woe;
Visions that come and go
Now haunt me constantly;
Firm and strong are my chains,
Nothing but death remains,
I can no more be free.

ON THY LIFE'S WAY.

—

ON thy life's way, may man be kind
    And help thee onward day by day;
May all prove friends that thou shalt find
        On thy life's way.

May thou in thy pathways wrong ne'er stray,
    And though to err thou'lt be inclined;
Remember always thou'rt but clay,
    And ever pray for strength of mind.
There's One above a constant stay,
    To whom thou should'st thy future bind—
        On thy life's way.

WORDS SAID IN RAGE.

—

WORDS said in rage are very seldom meant,
　　Though age notes keenly harshness by the young
　　For oft the hasty and impetuous tongue
Hurls out expletives that their anger sent.

Yet anger will have sway, and not content
　　With sentences so furiously flung—
　　They feel no pang that they their victims stung;
But then, in calmer moments they repent
　　　　　　Words said in rage.

Too late sometimes, the bitter seed is sown,
And to a plant of enmity has grown;
　　The venomed sting has sunk into the heart,
　　And friends for years are severed far apart;
Then they regret, and bitterly bemoan
　　　　　　Words said in rage.

WINTER.

—

RUDE Winter, with his withering hand,
 Has stretched fair Summer low;
And o'er the erstwhile beauteous land,
 With steady step and slow,
Has stripped the foliage from the trees
And plucked the flowerets from the leas.

Adown the valley, where the stream
 Made music sweet and clear,
He reigns, majestic and supreme,
 The monarch of the year—
Girt round with ice and chilling snow,
He blustering bids bold Boreas blow.

And on the hill-tops, where anon,
 All Nature seemed to smile,
With blighting breath has bade begone
 Their charms into exile.
How harsh his voice! his touch, how cold!
How dread, how drear, King Winter's fold.

A WEDDING FAVOUR.

NOW ye are bound by Heaven's most sacred tie,
  Linked each to each by love's most holy chain;
Oh! may the union earth's cares defy
  And prove a shield to soothe dull sorrow's pain.

Into our paths a little rain must fall,
  But sunshine comes anon, and drives away
The canker, and the trouble, and the gall,
  And once again shines out serenest day.

Bear ye each others burdens—life is brief!
  Kind words go far to ease the stricken heart.
Be just and fear not! God will send relief!
  Should sorrow pierce you with his poignant dart.

Then at the last when fleeting life in o'er,
  In realms e'er bright with pure unclouded rays,
You'll live Eternal on the Golden Shore,
  'Mid everlasting song of love and praise.

IN MEMORIAM

EDWIN WAUGH.*

———

THINE was the brilliant and the flowing pen,
   Bursting with gladness like the sparkling sea,
Mellow as music of the gentle streams
   And fragrant as the flowers upon the lea.

Thine was the minstrelsy we loved to hear,
   Thine was the light that hovered round our way,
Thine was the melody that thrilled the brain
   And spoke to us of one unending day.

But now, dear Waugh, thy spirit's passed away ;
   This sweet spring morning which thou loved so well,
Finds thee low-lying, 'neath the cold, cold clay—
   That narrow space, wherein all men must dwell.

On earth we loved to listen to thy voice ;
   It softly fell upon the wondering ear ;
How glad to think that in " the little while "
   We still may hear it in another sphere.

———

* Died April 30th, 1890, widely known in the North of England as the "Lancashire Burns."

TEDDY.

—

DEAR little Teddy, only five short years
    Had sped their path ere thou wert called away;
And now we long 'mid vain regret and tears
    For that glad morning when the break of day
Will find us with no cares—no pangs—no fears.

Could we once more have one sweet morning kiss,
    Or hear the ring of thy glad, boyish cheer,
'Twould be to us a taste of Heaven-sent bliss—
    For all thy words and all thy ways were dear,
And all thy antics, oh! we so much miss.

We little thought when watching thee at play
    That soon thy Lamp of Life would, flickering, die;
But oh! from ours has fled its brightest ray,
    For 'tis so hard, we say it with a sigh,
That thou'rt not with us this fair summer day.

Ah well! in God's good time, when gone has night,
    We too shall join thee in His house above,
Where all is sunny, and where pain and blight
    Never can enter, for there's nought but love
To dwell triumphant in His Realms of Light.

Morecambe, June 27th, 1890.

MARGUERITE.

—

DAINTY, tender, graceful, true,
Love,—my heart goes out to you.

Sweetness dwells within your heart,
God be praised—I have a part.

Loving, noble, gladsome, coy,
Blithesome ever for your boy.

Full of charms that glad the mind,
Ever trustful, brave and kind.

May your days be ever bright—
May you know no darksome night.

All your works and ways complete,
My own—my darling Marguerite.

Morecambe, July 10th, 1890.

AT THE GATE.*

—

BESIDE the gate once more I stand,
 Where Spring's fresh breeze my forehead fanned
 In days that now have fled—
When on it to and fro we swung,
For all was gay and life was young,
 And ne'er a tear was shed.

From here, we now, as could we then,
Behold the mossy, fern-clad glen,
 And daisy-spangled nook,—
Through here we went in childhood's hours,
Picking the bright and beauteous flow'rs,
 Down by the limpid brook.

* This poem was written in competition with one of the Author's most valued friends, after seeing a picture of " A Rustic Gate."

Ah! what a fairy sylvan scene,
When trees were dressed in living green,
   And birds sang loud and shrill;
When earth was crowned with golden bloom,
When neither sadness, care, nor gloom,
   Had tried our joy to kill.

My mem'ry still recalls the time,
Though thirty years I've passed my prime,
   When laughter's echoes sweet
Fill'd all the air with music gay
As thro' this gate we took our way
   With scamp'ring, boist'rous feet.

And gathered hawthorn berries bright,
Ah! they were treasures in our sight,
   None others could surpass—
Sometimes we plucked the wild, white rose,
Or, sudden tumble, would repose
   A moment on the grass.

Then up and chase the butterfly,
And thus, without a tear or sigh,
  Those gladsome moments went;
When neither anguish, grief nor pain
Disturbed the peace of youthful brain,—
  When bosoms were not rent

With grasp or greed for worldly things,
When time flew by on angels' wings
  And glory filled the earth;
When all was happiness and glee,
When all was love and harmony,
  And gladness hope and mirth.

But soon before another gate,
With all the holy, good, and great,
  Mayhap I'll have to stand;
And then I'll to the full rejoice,
When I can hear my Saviour's voice—
  "Enter the Better Land"!   F.

ONLY A GATE.

I STAND beside the rustic gate once more,
  The gate so full of memories to me ;
The intervening years are bridgéd o'er
  That have elapsed since boyhood's gaiety.

This time-worn gate brings back fair childhood's hours,
  My little comrades, happy as the day,
Who joined me in those fields to gather flowers.
  And wile away the happy hours in play.

But I have lost their faces long ago ;
  Their lives and mine have drifted year by year,
Further apart, and some are now laid low,
  Whilst I in retrospection linger here.

By that old gate sweet words of love were spoken,
  By me to one who should now be my wife ;
Here she received long years ago the token
  Of love—a ring—to bind our hearts for life.

Ah, lassie! could we only then have known,
    When heart to heart, we feared not time nor fate,
How soon our pleasant day-dreams would have flown,
    Should we have kissed so fondly by this gate?

Our hearts were true enough, our love was strong;
    The words sincere we uttered by this gate;
Pure our affection, we ne'er dreamt of wrong,
    But we were helpless in the hands of fate.

Dear lassie, never will I lay the blame
    Of all my lonely, weary years on thee;
Ne'er will I breathe but blessings on thy name,
    Tho' strangers now for ever we must be.

How oft at midnight have I lingered here,
    Dreaming sweet dreams of thee and future bliss,
Till, in my fancy, I could feel thee near,
    Responsive both to sweet caress and kiss.

And often, when in foreign, far-off climes,
    I've wandered lone at night to meditate,
Has memory conjured up those happy times
    We spent, my love and I, beside this gate.

Ah, memory! that leads us to the past,
   And shows us visions of the days long fled,
Thy pictures float across my vision fast
   In life again—as creatures from the dead.

Oh, past! with ever eager, open arms
   To clasp the present in thy embrace strong,
For thee no fears, no dread, no false alarms—
   All will be thine ; hush! hush! 'twill not be long.

Oh dreadful past, how fearful would'st thou be
   Had we no future for our better deeds !
Tho' memory always brings us straight to thee,
   Hope to a brighter future kindly leads.

Oh, past! the guardian of our long-lost day,
   The keeper of our secrets, of MY vow,
Thy door is locked ; e'en now I hear thee say,
   " Too late! too late ! ye cannot enter now."   G.

HARVEST.

'MOST every Bard delights to praise
    Glad Springtime's fresh and early days;
But now—though very dear is Spring,
Of her sweet charms I will not sing.
Autumn's blest, mellow joys divine,
Are now the dearest theme of mine;
So I will try to spin a rhyme,
To welcome days of Harvest-time.

The golden fields of waving corn,
Like sheep—seem waiting to be shorn;
How gay, how fresh, how fair they seem
All glittering 'neath the sun's glad gleam.
Whilst here, beneath the azure sky,
Serene in dreamy ease I lie;
And muse, as oft I've mused before
Of glorious harvest-days of yore.
I mind me well in days of old
Viewing with joy the fields of gold;

The reapers with the sickle keen
Mowing the bending blades of green;
The shocks of corn that busy hands
Have circled with their stalky bands;
The rustic cart, the village swain
Taking the bounteous store of grain;
The little stream, the rugged hill
The quaint old farm, the water mill;
The merry troop of children gay
Their lives, as yet, a holiday;
The gentle wind, the fluttering leaves
And all the joys that fancy weaves.

And then, when garnered is the grain,
When each field looks a barren plain;
How pleasant in the house of God,
To praise Him for the fruitful sod—
The gentle rain—the ripening sun
Which have such deeds of splendour done;
And for all blessings He has given
To thank the Lord of Earth and Heaven.

IN MEMORIAM.

J. T. B. Died July 11th, 1891.

—

WHAT though the shaft of death is hurled?
   'Tis God's good will!
He lives now in The Better World,
   Peace, then, be still.
Our Father's wisdom triumphs there,
And all is bright and free from care;
Let us then watch 'mid faith and prayer—
   Death cannot kill
The soul immortal. He who made
   This paltry clay,
Bids mortals not to be afraid
   Of that great day;
But so live here for evermore
That when we die our spirits soar
To highest Heaven's eternal shore—
   Far, far away.

RONDOLETS.

—

FAREWELL my own!
'Tis sad that we should have to part;
 Farewell my own;
And though I now am left alone
I have to cheer me, thy fond heart;
And yet, my love, the tear-drops start;
 Farewell my own.

 When we next meet—
From me no more thou'lt have to stray;
 When we next meet.
And ah! the joy when first we greet
On that sweet, joyous, halcyon day;
For with me thou wilt ever stay
 When next we meet.

UNDER THE OAK.

HERE it was our vows of love were spoken—
        Under the oak!
Here, alas! those self-same vows were broken;
        The words we spoke,
And the sweet hopes by our young hearts' begotten
        Were left to die;
To droop, to fade, neglected and forgotten—
        We knew not why.

Misunderstandings came, and we were parted;
        I went my way—
Dejected and forlorn and broken-hearted—
        In grief to stray.
And she went her path, maybe full of pity,
        At my hard yoke;
Mayhap, forget, 'mid life of busy city—
        Under the oak,

THE VILLAGE CHURCH.

GIRT round with waving elm trees
　Our village church still stands,—
With square embattled tower,
　Raised by our fathers' hands.

It is a shrine of glory
　To all the Saxon race,
Crowned o'er with clinging ivy,
　A fount of hallowed grace.

Its peaceful yard—God's acre—
　With many a grave is strewn;
Some, ta'en in serest lifetime,
　And some, alas! in June.

The older ones, forgotten,
　Neglected and forlorn;
The newer ones all radiant,
　From weed and refuse shorn.

Ah me! how very peaceful,
   Seemeth the holy fane;
'Tis God's own habitation
   Where He delights to reign.

'Tis one of His loved temples—
   Those glories of our land;
Where we can praise our Maker,
   And Sin and Death withstand.

Its crumblings walls are stately,
   Though falling to decay,
So time-worn and so honoured—
   So moss-grown o'er and grey.

I've known each stone since childhood,
   And love them each so well,
That now when gazing on them
   Comes o'er my soul a spell.

Once more 'tis merry Spring-time,
   Once more I am a child,
Gath'ring the buds and blossoms
   That Nature showers wild.

A laughing, prattling youngster
   With bound and romp and start,
No worldly cares about me,
   No pain within my heart.

Once more 'tis Sabbath morning,
   Again I worship here ;
I hear the vicar preaching,
   So earnest, firm, and clear.

My parents, too, are with me,
   Both in life's early prime ;
Both loving, true and tender—
   Ah! those were days sublime.

There comes another morning,
　The bells ring loud and sweet,
With swelling, joyous carols—
　Me and my bride to greet.

The children scattered flowers,
　The choir melodious sang;
Our hearts returned the rapture
　With ev'ry peal that rang.

But in the early winter
　Clangs out the solemn bell,
Grim-visaged death has claimed her,
　'Tis Mary's fun'ral knell.

Oh, soul, keep down thy madness,
　It is the King of Kings,
Who to His home has borne her
　And now with Him she sings.

Still comes another morning,
　　Oh, bosom wild, be still;
Remember He ordained it—
　　Bend to His holy will.

Within its sacred precincts,
　　Where years ago they wed—
No more again they'll praise Him,
　　For mother now is dead.

'Tis but a few weeks after—
　　The grave re-opens wide,
And they by death divided,
　　Are resting, side by side.

Ah me! the thought is bitter,
　　But God is ever just,
Tho' heart and mind are crying
　　Against the "Dust to dust."

I left my native village,
  To mem'ry ever blest—
I sought the city's babble,
  To ease my aching breast.

Vain deed! the throbbing city
  Relieved me not of care,
For life's best dreams had vanished—
  Remembrance lingered there.

I sailed the stormy ocean—
  In vain I looked for peace;
There came no hope to ease me,
  My yearnings would not cease.

I trod the mighty desert,
  And asked relief in prayer;
Methinks God sent me hither
  To soothe my bitter care.

My soul was filled with longings—
   For home 1 was athirst ;
For home and friends and kindred—
   My beating heart nigh burst.

And oh! with deep emotion—
   With mingled joy and pain—
I sought the shores of England
   To leave them ne'er again.

And now, all aged and wrinkled,
   I come to childhood's home,
1 wander through the village,
   Along its lanes 1 roam.

It softens my afflictions—
   1 need not further search ;
The tend'rest recollections cling
   Around the village church.

A NOBLE MAN.

A NOBLE man need not be made
   By fiat of a king's decree;
For we can find in every grade
          A noble man.

That man is noble who forbears
To scoff and jeer at daily prayers;
That man is noble, true and good
Who pays respect to womanhood;
That man is noble who refrains
To idly jest at others pains.
That man is noble, who says "trust
The God of Gods, for He is just."

A noble man no crest doth need,
   No grant of arms of quaint device;
He is—if right prompts every deed—
          A noble man.

THE WOOING.

I CANNOT woo thee calm and slow,—
  No sluggard love is mine;
There's madness in my pulses glow,
My blood is like the torrent's flow,
  O'erheated as with wine:
I feel a bliss which few can now
  When my hand's clasped in thine.

I now can hardly THINK thy name
  Without my throbbing heart
(A heart that monarchs cannot tame)
Burning like some volcanic flame
  With wild, tumultuous start;
And though I deem it not a shame—
Forgot are all my thoughts of fame,
  I thought would ne'er depart.

Ambition now is nought to me;
   Wealth, power, I do not crave ;
A freeman, yet no longer free,
For am I not enslaved by thee?
   Do I not of thee rave?
Am I not wrecked in love's fierce sea,
Whirling about tempestuously,
   Engulphed beneath its wave?

No coward fancy do I feel
   Mine's no illusioned brain,
Though oft it almost makes me reel—
For I am fettered o'er with steel,
   But thou canst break its chain ;
Lo! abject at thy feet I kneel,
And earnest ask, with wild appeal,
   For freedom once again.

Homage to thee for e'er I'll pay,
  My queen of love and light;
I'll be thy dog. and guard thy way,
Thy slave, thy servant, all the day
  Thy path shall aye be bright;
Oh! heed me as I humbly pray,
Say but the word—'twill shed its ray
  On my chaotic night.

Could'st thou but feel my passion's fire,
  Which rages fast within,
The flames which never will expire,
But glow more bright and always higher,
  When thee I strive to win;
Could st thou but feel love's keen desire,
Then would'st thou know that nought could tire
  My love's exhaustless bin.

Do I see on thy cheek the smile
    Which tells me I have won?
Thou dost not, then, my cause revile,
And though I've sunken 'neath thy wile,
    My pleadings dost not shun;
Ah! now I'm on a fairy isle,
With all things round me to beguile,
    And thou'rt my brightest sun.

I'll lavish on thee jewels rare!
    Of gold a boundless store;
I'll shield thee from earth's gentlest care
Thou shalt be fanned by zephyrs rare
    From some Elysian shore;
And day by day—as thou dost share
Thy life with mine, my angel fair,
    I'll love thee more and more.

LINES.*

COME lightsome breeze, with gentle kiss and low.
  And fan the fever from his heated brow ;
With kindly perfume, waft away the pain,
And make King Health o'er all his form to reign.
Blow soft and soothing, with a loving smile—
And all the weight from brain and heart beguile ;
Send sleep, good Morpheus, to wile his care,
And ye, blest Angels, watch o'er him with prayer ;
Make him refreshed and send him peaceful dreams,
Brightened and burnished by your Heavenly themes ;
And all ye fays whom magic potions give,
Offer to him each known restorative.
Ye sprites, his calmful slumbers still prolong,
And, when he wakes, renewed, and fresh, and strong,
Ours be the joy to swell a song of praise,
To Him who leads us through such devious ways ;
Ours be the bliss, our thanks to God to tend,
For His blest mercy to this noble friend.

CARMEN.

—

THE sunbeams kiss her golden hair,
  Which shimmers sparkling bright,
And falls in sweet entanglement
  On shoulders soft and white;
And an enraptured wonder,
  When you first see the sight,
Fills you with poet's melody
  When gazing on its light.

There seems to be a glory
  About her clear blue eyes.
Which 'minds you of some transient stream
  'Neath earth's cerulean skies;
Such orbs are only meant for mirth,
  And eloquent surprise,
Or to express the sunny smile
  Of love, that never dies;

For which the ancient minstrels,
   Their tuneful lyres would string,
And make the woodland air resound
   With its harmonious ring.
And on her marble forehead,
   Somehow there seems to cling
The same mysterious sweetness
   Of which Bards love to sing.

But to describe her fully
   Is quite beyond my reach ;
Sometimes her lips press firmly,
   At others they beseech ;
Like tiny corulets of pearl
   Her armaments of speech,
And cheeks as full of loveliness
   As blossoms of the peach.

Her maiden charms, however,
   Are not confined to face;
An elegance is in her step,
   Which adds unto her grace;
And where she goes she always lends
   Enchantment to the place—
For not a line of error
   In Carmen can you trace.

A SUMMER IDYL.

WHAT is this new, strange feeling
    That fills my soul with joy?
That over me comes stealing,
    And makes me feel so coy?
That thrills my bosom and my heart
    With most divine romances,
And causes all my frame to start
    With most delicious fancies.

And why do all the lovely flowers
    Each wear a brighter hue?
And why do all the passing hours
    Seem sadly short and few?
Why does my heart seem lighter?
    What makes my pulses glow?
What makes the world seem brighter?
    I really do not know.

Why do my cares seem fewer?
    What makes all earth so gay!
The very sky seems bluer
    Than this time yesterday.
The birds they sing more sweetly,
    The gaudy butterflies
Come near me indiscreetly,
    The thrush melodious cries.

And onward flows the river,
    As though from care set free,
So calm, without a quiver
    It glides on to the sea.
And now the stars are shining
    And twinkling up afar:
Each set in golden lining—
    Like me—no gloom to mar.

They seem to shine more brilliantly
 Than this time yester-night;
Or, perhaps, it is to only me
 They look more dazzling bright.
But only one short day has passed.
 Since Jack proposed to me;
Will each seem fairer than the last,
 More full of harmony?

My work to-day went quick and smooth,
 At noon I was not tired;
Perhaps the ring he gave me soothed
 (The ring I so admired).
Methinks I feel his warm, sweet kiss
 Now burning on my face;
Jack said I was his dearest bliss—
 That I was full of grace.

And then we told the story
   Oft told in days of yore;
And now the earth holds glory
   It never held before.
Ah me! I must have been asleep
   Till last night by the lake,
And Jack asked for my heart to keep,
   I found myself awake.

Into my soul there seems to be
   A feeling so sincere,
A heavenly blend of sweetest glee
   Has come my heart to cheer!
None saw us in the gloaming,
   None heard but the stars above;
I think it's my brain that's roaming,
   But Jack says it is 'love.'

LET US BE GAY.

LET us be gay and full of glee,
    And drive dull care and grief away ;
Let us be happy as can be—
        Let us be gay.

Let all our pent-up mirth be free,
   Let us give vent to fun and play;
Let us delight in all we see,
   Let us be careless as the day;
Let us sing glad and joyfully
   Some sweet, soul-stirring roundelay;
Let us rouse moorland, wood, and lea—
        Let us be gay.

DOWN BY THE BROOK.

—

DOWN by the brook I sat to rest
    And muse on Natures open book;
The glorious day was at its best—
                Down by the brook.

The woods, in garb of green were drest,
    And had to me a pleasant look;
The far blue hills adown the west
    Seemed beauteous from this lovely nook,
For Summer was their welcome guest
    And from them winter's robe had shook;
All told of her sweet interest—
                Down by the brook.

RAIN.

SOFTLY, gently, falls the rain.
    Pattering on the window pane,
'Freshing Nature's fairest bowers,
Moistening all the drooping flowers.

Making every tree robust,
Quenching many a cloud of dust;
Giving earth a glorious feast,
Finding drink for man and beast.

Running down a thousand hills,
Filling up a thousand rills ;
Falling with a tender care,
Clearing all the drowsy air.

Gladdening mountain, wood and plain;
Brightening everything again ;
Cheering, with its welcome showers,
All the sultry summer hours.

OLD LOVE.

—

NOT long ago
  I met my fate ;
They call her Kate !
And you must know
My face doth glow,
 For here I wait
  With mind elate
My love to show.

This charming maid
  Has all my heart ;
  We ne'er shall part,
Don't be afraid !
  And. do not start ;
She's 'old and staid,'
  She's fifty-four,
  And I'm three score.

THE PLEBEIAN PATRICIAN.*

—

FILLED with vague longings that can ne'er be
        granted,
  Yearning to leave his footprints on time's sands;
Wondering and wishing, while his poor heart panted,
  If he with 'men of blood' would e'er shake hands.
Watts' motto nought to him, for ne'er on earth
Can he prove lineage long, and ancient birth.

His blood runs coursing through his red-hot veins
  With all the mad, tempestuous rage of youth;
He lacks not strength, yet counts he all his gains
  But bitter loss, for knows he not the truth?
Who is he?   A mere unit on this sphere,
And when he's gone, who'll know he e'er was here.

---

* This is one of the Author's earlier efforts, and, he would point out, purely imaginary.

He waits and hopes in vain to make a name,

 Trusting that, unforseen, some chance may come

By which the annals of recorded fame

 May bear his brand—but fame for him is dumb!

He works and waits, but weary grows his mind

In seeking for this bubble undefined.

It is nought to him that the world is fair,

He is weighted down with his load of care;

His heart and his brain grow heavy and sad,

His grief and his care almost drive him mad,

He cannot hope with the elite to mate—

And he mourns and grieves at his own-made fate;

His mind is racked and his body is worn,

He is downcast and hopeless, wretched, forlorn;

He's wrinkled and haggard before his time,

As though burdened o'er with a fearful crime;

His eyes are bleared and his hair is gray,

And when night-time comes he longs for the day;

When the day is here he wishes for night,

The future to him seems a fearful blight

The life he now leads is a living tomb--

And little he cares for the Summer's bloom;

Spring-time and Harvest-time no charms unfold,
He is yearning for rank and not for gold,
His bosom glows wild with a flame of fire—
To grow cool and chill with his mad desire :
His frame is feeble and each tottering limb
Shows to the world the folly of his whim.

Now reason starts to falter,
    All is an endless crave,
This feeling ne'er will alter—
    On this side of the grave.

Still, still his wild unreasoning,
    For ever holds its sway,
And 'tis as strong at even
    As at the dawn of day.

Now lunacy's strange babblings
    Enfolds him in its arms ;
His thirst for old nobility—
    No longer holds its charms.

His brain grows more enfeebled,
   And scarce has strength to think;
It now seems overhanging
   The dreaded Stygian brink.

But still as fancy leads it,
   And reason seems to glow,
There comes this strange meandering
   That now is cool and slow: —

Open, ye doors, and enclose me within,
I'm guiltless as ye, nor am tarnished with sin,
Let me once enter a nobleman's hall,
Join in your mirth as of old did King Saul!
List to my longing, give heed to my cry,
Grant my request and in peace I can die.
I long once to see your spear-covered walls,
To tread on your floors, your oaken-carved halls,
From your turrets to see the fair world beneath,
Meadow and pasture, and thyme-scented heath;
Let me enter the place where knights of the blood,
And peers of the realm, and princes have stood;
Let me sit at your board and eat bread with ye

Join your repast and be one of the free !
Just let me once see your arms and your crest,
Then I will gladly sink down to my rest.

    BUT all away they turn him
      Not one to him will list,
    The servants ever spurn him—
      His voice is always hissed.

    But now the end approaches,
      There comes a feeling dense—
    A dull and heavy feeling—
      O'erbearing and intense.

    His pulse has nigh stopped beating!
      His flesh grows hard and cold!
    His life away is fleeting!
      Grim death has taken hold:

And now he rests in that calm tranquil cell,
Where peer and peasant—rich and poor must dwell;
Where all are equal—for King Death's embrace
Respects not rank, nor blood, nor noble race;

When his harsh voice bids flickering life to cease
'Tis no use asking for a longer lease.
Why then the crave for noble ancestry?
For pomp and show of glittering pageantry?
These things are lent but for the little while,
Good deeds are often done by "rank and file."
We all can trace our being from the sod,
We're all alike to the immortal God!

*TO PROF. R. B. WINDER, M.D. D.D.S.

AND THE MEDICAL FACULTY OF THE BALTIMORE

COLLEGE OF DENTAL SURGERY.

—

TEN thousand thanks, ye men of learning vast,

To deem me worthy of such radiant honour ;

To stamp me with your brilliant document—

Which much before all other things I prize.

When this distinction ye confer on me

I feel the deeds I've done scarce merit it ;

Yet in the future I will struggle on !

And, like the thirsty flowers revivified

By gentle showers of sweet nutritious rain—

---

* On receiving from that time-honoured Institution the Honorary Degree of Doctor
of Dental Surgery.   Thinking it may interest some of his readers the Author
quotes the following from the latest edition of the College Calendar. "The oldest and first
of Dental Colleges, this Institution enters on the fiftieth year of its career, with its prospects
for usefulness brighter than ever before. It has added to its Faculty and Medical Corps
strong and active men, and is better equipped than at any period of its existence. The result
of its work in these fifty years are world-wide in their influence upon Dentistry. Fourteen
hundred and twenty-seven graduates have gone from this College into practice, and these are
scattered all over the civilized world. They are located in nearly every City of Europe. They
lead the profession in all the great centres of civilization, and have won eminence and renown
in England, France, Russia, Prussia, Switzerland, Spain and Italy. They have carried the
honours of the Institution into Asia, Australia, and the land of the Pyramids, while in every
State in the United States they have established their own worth and the reputation of their
Alma Mater. The College may well point with pride to the standing of its graduates. Many
of them have reached high stations in their profession ; many have become renowned for their
attainments, original discoveries and writings. They have met with signal honour abroad,
nearly every Court Dentist in Europe being a graduate of this Institution. Very many of
these are men of broad culture, who had been previously trained in other high educational
institutions, and, collectively they have developed a degree of worth and usefulness which
reflects the highest credit upon the College. No effort will be spared to give the Baltimore
College of Dental Surgery the highest rank among like Institutions, as it was the pioneer of
Dental education in the world"—Honorary Degrees are only granted to distinguished
members of the profession—and, without fee.

My mind will have an ever present thought,
That thought will be—Oh! noble men, and true,
Of this great dignity, that to me ye grant.
And should I, like some countrymen of yours,
E'er rise to world-wide fame, or high renown,
I shall attribute—more to this kind act
Than any deed that thought of mine could do.
And I will labour on—my vigour 'freshed
And warmed—and if in future days there comes
An inspiration from the realms divine
Such as has ne'er before been granted man;
Then shall I speak with a triumphant voice,
And far-forgetting past and present works
Shall sing to you—in science justly famed,—
Deep from my heart, a swelling song of praise.
No feeble lay—no theme that other men
Have dealt with—but a soul-stirring song
Original and powerful to the last;
Shining with each attribute of the Muse—

Glowing with energy—distinct and clear,
Glittering like gems in some chaotic world,
That, may be, will lead some from desert paths
Into a day serene with rapturous light.
And though I breathe this strain—'twill not be mine,
I merely am the soil that brings it forth !—
Ye have implanted it, and nourished it,
And all the credit I will freely give
To you—so full of generous impulses—
I would be strong in right; this recognition
If ever such there be—is justly earned;
For, known and famed in almost every clime,
Baltimore College is pre-eminent—
Its graduates are admired in every land,
Its teachers all, are learnéd men, and good,
Famous and acknowledged in each sphere,
Eminently fitted for their post of trust.
They well become the College of their choice,
And are a credit to a learned profession.

Would that my halting pen could do it now,
Would that the coyful muse would cool my brow,
And my brain fill with blest prefulgency,
So that I might describe my ecstasy.
The mind is willing but its power is weak !
Still there shall come a time when it will speak !
My words shall in the loudest tones be hurled
    With force and ardour I will them invest,
    And praise my Alma Mater—largest, best,
And oldest Dental College in the World.

FORGET THEE?

FORGET thee!   Can the youth forget
   His first and only love?
Forget thee!   Can the stars forget
  To shine in Heaven above?

Forget thee!   Can the morn forget
   To give her radiant light?
Forget thee!   Can the moon forget
   To shed her beams at night?

Forget thee!   Can the flowers forget
   To bloom 'neath Summer sun?
Forget thee!   Can the brook forget
   To blithely onward run?

Forget thee! Can the rain forget
  To fall in plenteous showers?
Forget thee! Can the dew forget
  To brighten drooping flowers?

Forget thee! Can the snow forget
  To fall in Winter time?
Forget thee! Can the Bard forget
  To tell his thoughts in rhyme?

Forget thee! Can the child forget
  To frisk and romp at play?
Forget thee! Can the bride forget
  This is her marriage day?

Forget thee! Can the trees forget
  To don their dress in Spring?
Forget thee! Can the birds forget
  To flit on lightsome wing?

Forget thee! Can the waves forget
　　To ripple on the shore?
Forget thee! Can the sea forget
　　To hush its mighty roar?

Forget thee! Can the wind forget
　　To sob or scream at will?
Forget thee! Can the world forget
　　To evermore be still?

Ah, no! they never can forget,
　　And I forget not thee;
And all the happy times we met
　　And locked in my memory.

ADVICE.

BANISH ever from the heart
   Jealousy's forbidding seeds;
Let your actions aye impart
   Others to still brighter deeds.

Bid begone the tempter's voice—
   Drive away all bitterness;
Try and make some soul rejoice
   Give them half your happiness.

Weed all angry words away,
   Curb the power of hasty tongue,
Forget the hurts of yesterday,
   Pardon every foe his wrong.

A LOST LOVE.

—

BE still mad heart, and cease thy wild, vain beatings;
   Grow cool, thou throbbing brain, and let me think;
I came not here to take her gladsome greetings,
   For long ago she crossed the dreaded brink.

What did I come for—why this vain returning?
   Ah me! my bosom feels a bitter pain;
I came to satisfy intensest yearning—
   I came to see my loved one's home again.

The pangs are mine—pangs of severest sorrow—
   The grief is mine—a grief that still holds sway—
For well I know earth holds no bright to-morrow
   To clear the darkness from each gloomy day.

No comfort comes with kindly hand caressing—
   No joys approach to ease my poignant lot—
Nought comes to cheer my night of dark distressing,
   Nought can I hear but her " Forget-me-not."

These words she spoke when to High Heaven ascending,
   And I can ne'er forget her last farewell!
I know—I feel—my grief will know no ending
   Until my soul doth with my loved one's dwell.

LIFE'S CHANGES.

AT TWENTY EIGHT.

—

I AM young and strong !
But youth cannot last for aye—
 And my strength will fly
 As the years roll by ;
Until there shall come a day.
 Be it soon or long,
When my spirit must pass away.

 To-day I feel sad,
That a thing like age should be;
 And my heart rebels,
 And my anger swells,
That youth cannot dwell with me ;
 I cannot be glad
At this grim reality.—

AT SIXTY-EIGHT.

I AM old and weak!
Yet it seems but yesterday
    I was young and strong;
    But the years flew along,
And now I am nearing the day,
    And it seemeth not bleak,
When my spirit must pass away.

    What changes time brings!
All sadness is turned to joy;
    And my thankful heart
    Has never a smart
Its gratefulness to cloy;
    For my spirit sings
Of Life which Time cannot destroy.

FAREWELL.

—

I HAVE been with you both in joy and care,
  Through many paths together we have strayed,
And I have found some gladness everywhere—
  On barren moor and in the forest shade.

If ye have shared my gladness and delight,
  My rapture is the deeper, and my joy
Will never fade until life's darksome night
  Doth all my memory's happy links destroy.

Together we have roamed on sunny ways,
  Together trod the clouded path of life;
I am content if these my humble lays
  Have soothed and softened sorrow's sordid strife.

TRIBUTARY POEMS.

*YORKSHIRE.

AN ODE TO DR. FORSHAW.

THERE'S grandeur in the wild old Yorkshire hills;
  There's beauty in her rivers, brooks and rills;
There's mystery in her ancient rocks and caves,
Her rude old cromlechs and her barrowed graves;
There's music in her woods and flowery dells,
Her gurgling streams, cascades and dropping wells;
And in her Abbeys, Minsters, Castles, all—
Though clinging ivy crowns each crumbling wall,
We see and read, with thoughts that make us start,
Historic scenes, and skill in antique art,—
All these—as with a living sunset glow
Have filled thy soul to running overflow;
And fanned to flame the true poetic fire
That lingered, slumbering, in thy tuneful lyre.
Sing on—and may the Naiads and the nine
Attune thy heart to swell with tones divine.

                    Rev. JOHN W. KAYE, M.A. LL.D.
            Author of *The Lives of the Wives of the Poets, &c.*

---

* Reprinted from " The Enniskillen Reporter."

A SONNET*

TO DR. C. F. FORSHAW.

—

THOU genial Bard! Still write thy verses sweet,
  And give us glimpses of the days of yore ;
Pour forth the gems of thy poetic store,
  Thy countless readers' hearts with joy to greet.
May each fair daughter of Mnemosyne
  Come to thy aid and elevate thy song,
And in especial the sweet Euterpe.
  Thy swelling strains of minstrelsy prolong.
Write on, sweet Bard, and to us freely give
Thy gems poetic—they will ever live
  In countless generations yet unborn ;
Write on ; thy pen by poet's fancy led,
Thy thoughts will live when thou art with the dead,
  Awaiting welcome to a brighter morn.

JOSEPH GAUNT, B.A. B.Sc.
Author of *Eventide*, &c. &c.

—

* Reprinted from the " Leeds Times."

TO C. F. FORSHAW, ESQ.. LL.D.*

GOD'S gift to human kind are manifold!
  To one He gives the "tongue of flame" to wake
The woe-worn peasant from his bondage old;
  To one the "cunning hand," from clay to make
Forms whose rare beauty strikes beholders mute;
  To one the power the subtlest sounds to weave
Into sweet harmonies to conquer man and brute.
  To one, the will heroic to achieve
Deeds pregnant with the seeds of future good;
  Each has his mission, working to one goal,
But he stands nearest to the giver—God—
  Whose gift it is to teach the human soul
THROUGH SONG, the world is beautiful and fair,
And Heaven can but be reached by virtue, faith and
    prayer.

This is the poet's mission, loftier none,
Still keep thou true to this, thy fame is won.

G. T. LAWLEY,
Author of The History of Bilston, &c. &c.

---

* Reprinted from the "Midland Weekly News."

*TO MY FRIEND, CHAS, F. FORSHAW, LL.D.

In memory of pleasant hours spent over Poetic labours.

—

PLEASANT thoughts, and pleasant mem'ries,
    Are within the soul enshrined,
When we think o'er all the pleasures
    We have treasured far behind.
Pleasures which our dreams awaken'd
    'Neath the spell of friendship's smile,
When together up fame's mountain
    Fancy bore us free from guile.

Pleasant dreams and pleasant musings,
    O'er fame's battles yet unwon ;
Castles built in fairy airland
    'Neath ambition's fitful sun.
Gladsome dreams of coming glory,
    Laurel wreaths and joys uncrown'd,
Some laments, and some recallings,
    When dame fortune, weeping, frown'd.

' Reprinted from the "Staffordshire Knot."

When our souls together blended
   In the rich poetic thought,
Felt we not like beings enchanted
   'Neath the inspiration caught ?
Felt we not the tender passions
   Which the heart alone can feel,
When the inmost depths of reason
   Could not long the fire conceal ?

Ah! the hours we've spent together
   In the old, old pleasant days,
Are like sungleams 'mid life's shadows,
   Beacon lights beyond the haze.
Hopes that fill the cup of pleasure
   With the dews of early morn,
Making souls athirst for friendship,
   Longing for new joys unborn.

JAMES MUNDY,
Author of *Echoes from the Realm of Thought*·

TO DR. FORSHAW.*

MY much esteemed and new-found friend,
 A kind acknowledgment I send
To thank you for the lines you've penned
   About my humble self.

I feel in duty bound to you,
In honest truth I ought to do,
And send this rude spun line or two
   To stow upon the shelf.

But if you think it worth the while
To bring it into rank and file ;
And though perhaps not the best of style
   You're welcome so to do.

My brother Bards I love ye all,
Although our fame is yet but small ;
I hope no harm will e'er befall,
   Nor come to me or you.

* Reprinted from " Yorkshire Poets."

So here's my heart, and here's my hand,
Firm as the truth united stand
And wave aloft our magic wand
      In this new enterprise.

All honour to our leading man
Who guides the "Yorkshire Poets" van,
May each and all do what they can;
      In public favour rise.

Though some may laugh and others sneer,
Hold up your heads and never fear;
Though critics use their dart and spear,
      True worth will ever shine.

Then let us on together jog,
Steer clear of all the mist and fog,
Be wary of the treacherous bog
      That may engulph the Nine.

JOHN EMSLEY, F.S.A.
Author of *Rural Musings*, 1883.

TO A BROTHER BARD.

—

THANKS, Poet friend, for sympathy so sweet,
    It sheds of joy, upon life's path, a ray,—
It sweetens life, and cheers one on his way,—
It makes the bond of union more complete
When with a sympathy sincere you greet
    A brother toiler, sinking 'neath his load,
    Trudging along, uncertain of his road,
You out upon life's pathway chance to meet.

Sweet singer—brother bard—to-day, to thee
I send thee this, my New Year's offering;
And though, may be, in falt'ring notes I sing,
    Accept my gift—though feeble it may be,
And if "home-spun"—yet from a heart sincere
I wish both thee and thine a glad New Year.

    THOMAS BILSBOROUGH, F.G.S., Edin.
        Vice-President "Yorkshire Literary Society."

*TO DR. CHAS. F. FORSHAW,
PRESIDENT OF THE YORKSHIRE LITERARY SOCIETY.

Dear Doctor,

BRANDED together with one common aim—
  The good of others solely our intent—
Non nobis solum blazoned on our crest
  We hail thee then, as our first President.

It is not often in this mundane world
  That merit such as thine meets due reward,
But they who know thee best think otherwise
  And would assist thee rather than retard.

Though highly elevated once again,
  Be just and firm, true to thy self as well—
Act well thy part, that so in after years
  Thou mayest with pleasure on past actions dwell.

But, in the coming year be thou prepared,
  Thou canst not please, nor satisfy each one—
Do thou thy duty fearlessly, and then
  It can be said thy work was nobly done.

I am, Dear Doctor, thine with all regard
A fellow member, and a would-be Bard.

THOMAS BILSBOROUGH, F.G.S. Edin.

* Reprinted from " Yorkshire Poets."

TO DR. C. F. FORSHAW.*

(On reading his poem "Figures in the Fire.")

—

DEAR loving eyes
  That look with holy light
On all things sad,
On all things bright;
That glisten when they see
The good that's done
On land and sea
When Faith's great battle's won.

That watch tired feet
Tread holy paths,
And long to see
The drunkard's home
Changed to a haven
For help, as guide and light
The laugh with hearty glee
Where children's lightsome frolic be.

---

* Reprinted from the "Yorkshire Weekly Post."

Bright eyes that use their light
In trying to ease
The tottering steps of Age,
When weakened by sad sorrow's breeze
That light with smiles
Which oft beguiles
The would-be weary hours
That ruthless Pain may wage.

Oh! may your light
For long be bright,
Which earth's sorrow ne'er can dim;
And may life's closing hymn
Be as great Goethe's
When earth passes from your sight—
By loving. sorrowing hearts be sung
And see the light, more light.

EDWARD WALTON.

*TO DR. CHAS. FORSHAW.

—

TO pen my thanks I oft have tried,
And to the muse in vain I've sighed,
       Then closed the book;
But now I must some tribute send
To one whom I esteem a friend,
       To whom I look.
I would in some small measure send
My song of hearty thanks to blend
       With that of thine;
And if, for friendly aid bestowed,
Hearts ever thankfully have glowed,
       E'en so doth mine.
As staff to pilgrim on the road,
As happy song to those that brood,
       Some comfort given,
So hast thou ta'en a helping part
With hand and word, and from the heart
       Hast sadness driven.

                    HERBERT L. BOOTH,
                       Author of *Poems*. 1886.

* Reprinted from the "Ilkston Observer."

TO DR. FORSHAW.

YOUR book I've read with much regard—
   I hope you'll meet your just reward.
Our money spent in works like these,
Is sure to instruct, amuse and please.
Worthy of Emperor, Queen, or King,
To each of these I know you sing
In songs so sweet, so grand, so good,
They are the richest mental food,
They will instruct, improve the mind
And be a friend to all mankind;
They teach us to respect each other
And be to all men, friend and brother.
They help us onward evermore,
To aye be just and God adore.

                        WILLIAM EVANS,
                           Author of *Poems*, 1885.

TO CHAS. F. FORSHAW, LL.D.

——

"A swap o' rhymin ware
Wi ane anither."—BURNS.

——

DEAR Doctor, after much delay
    My book to you I send,
And at the outset let me say
    I send it to a friend.

For who can read your fervid lines
    And in them fail to find
The glowing zeal that in them shines?
    The love for human kind!

The heaven-born power that prompts the heart
    To further human weal,
Doth to the soul a peace impart
    The pen can ne'er reveal.

In heart and mind I've been with you
   Through Nature's lovely maze;
Seen e'en the simple drop of dew
   Glow with its Maker's praise.

When on my books my eyes I feast,
   As they stand side by side;
Your volume, sir, is not the least
   I view with honest pride.

"My book I'll give for yours," you said,
   We struck the bargain there;
And yours, under the terms so made,
   To me is doubly dear.

To spend an hour with you I'll try,
   I cannot tell you when, sir;
But I'll come over by-and-bye—
   Yours truly, RICHARD SPENCER.

                    Author of *Field Flowers*, 1890.

* TO DR. FORSHAW, M.A.

—

HAIL! Noble poet of our glorious shire!
   In whom doth burn the true poetic-fire;
Thou hast given to us many a dainty lay—
Of themes romantic— scenes of every day—
Which thou observing with a poet's eye,
Invests with charms of graceful fantasy;
No rhymes too difficult for thy agile muse,
Thou dost in all some truth and grace infuse.
Nor does mere fame content thy ardent soul,
For with intent to increase thy county's roll,
Of honourable men, in deeds, or song, or lore,
Thou, wandering by the wayside hedge or moor,
Hast culled poetic wildflowers, many a lovely one
Which set in *Yorkshire Poets* are as sunflowers to thy sun.

LAURA HALLIDAY·

* Reprinted from the " Midland Weekly News."

TO DR. C. F. FORSHAW, LL.D.

*On hearing that he was collecting *The Poets of the Spen Valley*, 1891.

———

MOST worthy Forshaw ; thine be all the praise,
    For putting in book form our humble lays ;
Our God we praise, for minds so cute and terse :
Who pen their thoughts, and put them into verse,
And entertain their friends, in such a way,
Instruct their minds, and noble thoughts convey.
Long may thy powers of mind and thought be spar'd
To create joys in verse, by others shared.
My gratitude I give thee, and sincerely trust ;
Thy efforts may be crowned when we are in the dust.

                    JOHN ODDY.

* See page 254.

* TO DR. CHAS. F. FORSHAW.

SUGGESTED BY HIS "FIGURES IN THE FIRE."

I AM calmly sitting and watching the firelight rise and
    fall

On the old familiar wainscot and the pictures 'gainst
    the wall,

When a tiny gleam comes flickering over the embers
    bright,

And, somehow, it stirs my heartstrings with a glad
    and strange delight;

For I am a little child once more, and sit by a
    mother's knee,

And that tiny gleam lighteth up with love the face
    so dear to me.

Then a huge blaze flickers, then rises, above that
    tiny light

And sweet is the dream of youthful days that falls
    upon my sight;

For mem'ry bringeth thoughts of youth when my life
    was bright and gay—

When my heart was filled with hope and love, and
    life like summer's day

All passed too soon; yet I linger now on the days so
    sweet to me,

As fancy lendeth her gladsome aid, and a lover's
    form I see.

---

* Reprinted from the " Yorkshire Weekly Post."

Then cometh a crash of embers, and my glad day-
dream is o'er,

For my lover's form hath vanished, and my heart is
sad and sore—

Ah, life! with thy changeful shadows, my day-dreams
have turned to night,

Nothing is left to touch my heart with a glad and
strange delight,

As alone I sit and watch the light that flickers to
and fro,

For nought remains but a memory of the days of
long ago.

For I'm a spinster old, sitting here in the flick'ring
light,

Yet sweet the dreams of happy days that have passed
before my sight;

For though life-like, the ember's glow is swiftly
passing away,

I shall meet the forms I love at the close of my
winter's day—

For I know that though they have passed from me
their souls are pure and white,

I am purer—nearer to them, for the dreamland fancies
to-night.

Mrs. R. H. BILSBOROUGH.

TO DR. CHAS. F. FORSHAW, LL.D.

On hearing that the Honorary Degree of Doctor of Dental Surgery
had been conferred on him by the Baltimore
College of Dental Surgery.

IF e'er a thought can stir the soul within,
    Or cause the breast to swell with honest pride,
It is when honours fall amid the din
    Of fervent battle on life's rapid tide.
Thy one desire has found deservéd fame
    Amid the countless dangers of the fray,
For thou hast earned thyself an honour'd name
    In spite of all that calumny may say.

Amidst the throng of those whose dreams aspire
    To reach ambition's far-off shining goal,
Thy works and deeds have fann'd the glowing fire
    And caught the spark which animates the soul.
The fountain head of Dental learnéd lore—
    Inspired by glory, reason's light has shed—
Has honour'd thee from famous Baltimore
    And placed their laurel wreath upon thy head.

I honour those who honour friend of mine,
    And sing the praises of the noble men
Who mete reward for labour such as thine;
    Can worthier theme inspire a Poet's pen?

Can worthier thought enrich the soulful lay,
  Or animate the sweet melodious lyre?
Can richer words the bond of love display
  Than those which bid a friend to 'step up higher.'

I dub thee Doctor—honour'd poet-friend—
  The proud distinction thou hast newly won
Should e'en enrich thy muse's favour'd end,
  And fill the air with reason's voice "well done."
This new Degree should bring thee great renown,
  And place thee high in future's noble grade,
Should bid thee fear no *confrere's* jealous frown
  But help thee woo the smile of fortune's aid.

All honour to the men of Baltimore!
  The Institution first and oldest known,
Though seas divide us from their fertile shore—
  We laud the great and honour'd name they own.
We waft a message on the western breeze
  From thankful hearts to dignify the same;
We feel a pride that favours such as these
  Should fall on Dr. Forshaw's well-earned fame.

JAMES MUNDY,
Secretary "Yorkshire Literary Society."

Published Works

BY

CHAS. F. FORSHAW, LL.D.

Wanderings of Imagery. A volume of Poems.
72 pp. 1886. 1/-.

Thoughts in the Gloaming. A volume of Poems·
60 pp. 1887. 1/-.

Poems. 304 pp. 1889. 3/-.

Yorkshire Sonneteers, to be completed in six volumes.
Vol. 1, 1889, being Sonnets and Biographies by Yorkshire Sonnet
Writers. 2/6.

Yorkshire Poets, Past and Present, to be completed in six volumes. 192 pp. Vols. I, II, III and IV now ready,
1888, 1889, 1890, 1891. Issued in monthly parts at 1/6 per annum, or
bound in half calf price, 5/- per vol. Illustrated.

The Poets of Keighley, Bingley and District.
200 pp. Being Biographies and Poetry of various Bards, natives or
residents of the above districts. Illustrated. 2/6. 1891.

**The Wild Boar of Cliffe Wood, or How
Bradford got its Crest.** 12 pp. 1886.

The Village Wedding: A Poem. 1888. Dedicated
to Sir Wm. Christopher Leng.

My Little Romance. A Novelette. 1891.

The Life of Hannah Dale. (For private circulation
only.) 1888.

Special Constableship in Bradford. 16 pp.
1890.

**A Short History of Tobacco, with its Effect
on the General Health and its Influence on the
Teeth.** 20 pp. 1887. (Over a million copies have been sold.)

Alcohol: Its Use and Abuse. 16 pp. Being a
Lecture delivered at the Bankfoot Mutual Improvement Society ;
Alderman Morley, J.P., Mayor of Bradford, in the chair. 1889.

The Teeth and How to Save Them. Being a
Lecture delivered before the Bradford Parish Church Young Men's
Society, the Rev. Canon Bardsley, D.D. Vicar of Bradford, in the
chair. 40 pp. 1885.

**Hints to Parents on the Management of
their Children's Teeth.** 12 pp. 1890.

Stammering, its Causes and its Cure. Written
by request for the Dental Section of the Ninth International Medical
Congress, held at Washington, U.S.A. 1887.

Cocaine, for Tooth Extraction. 1891. Reprinted
from the "Cleckheaton Guardian."

PRESS OPINIONS

On Dr. FORSHAW'S last Volume of Poems.

⇢ₒᵢ⇠

The LEEDS MERCURY says

" Chiefly lyrics, these verses, by a busy professional man, show close sympathy with nature. The poems on places and the domestic verses are especially fine, but here and there, as in ' The Soldier's Story ' and ' Lady Bell,' we have indication that Dr. Forshaw has in him a good share of the power and skill of the ballad writer. He is a diligent student, some of his poems possessing a rare touch of humour. There is a sprinkling of love ditties, and indeed, there are few phases of versification to which Dr. Forshaw does not turn, and, as a rule, with pleasing results. The volume entitles him to an advanced place among our leading Yorkshire Poets."

The LEEDS TIMES says :—

" Everywhere is seen the cultivated mind, the clear intellect, and the divinely born afflatus, for which thousands in our land have sighed and sighed in vain. Dr. Forshaw is a veritable sweet singer. His harp is attuned to the music of nature, and to the clear and heaven-born sounds from which the inspiration of the true poet is drawn. No one can read any of the poems in the volume before us, without being wiser and better than before ; and the best of it is that the spring from whence inspiration is drawn seems to be like the never-failing clear rill running down the mountain side, independent alike of storm or flood, or wind or rain—or indeed of any sublunary influence whatever. The volume will be welcome in many a quiet nook and corner of our land, and cannot fail to bring its author high renown."

The DEWSBURY CHRONICLE says :—

" Its perusal has been a pleasure and a profit, the general freshness in the treatment of the poems fascinates the reader and rivets his attention. It is a book that we can confidently recommend, and is sure to raise its author to the front rank of the minor poets of England and to ensure him a place amongst the few Yorkshire bards whose names will be honoured long after the present generation has passed away."

The WAKEFIELD HERALD says :—

" Dr. Forshaw's poems are written in varying metres, but all have a harmonious swing that doubles the pleasures of reading them. They are worthy of a wide circulation, and ought to obtain an extensive one throughout the country."

The ILKLEY GAZETTE says:—

" To go through them one by one, and quote the many expressive and beautiful passages would be to fill a column or two of excellent quotations which any writer would only too gladly have at his finger ends."

The BARNSLEY CHRONICLE says:—

" It will secure for him a permanent place in the ranks of Yorkshire literary worthies."

The SHEFFIELD TELEGRAPH says:—

" Dr. Forshaw's poems are specially interesting. They display considerable ability in poetical and metrical composition."

The STAFFORDSHIRE KNOT says:—

" It is a splendid memorial of the author's genius. His thoughts are fine and lofty. From its perusal the reader will get much real enjoyment, and some food for strong, good thought.

The BRADFORD ILLUSTRATED WEEKLY TELEGRAPH says:—

" I notice in ' Popular Poets of the Period'—a London publication— a sketch of the life of Dr. Forshaw, who is a regular contributor to Poet's Corner of this paper; also several of his poems which have appeared in our columns. Dr. Forshaw is to be congratulated that his poems are thought worthy of a place in the same volume as Tennyson, Browning, Swinburne, Rosetti, G. R. Sims, Prof. Blackie, Alfred Austin, Dr. Mackay, Newsam, and all the first poets of the day.

The BRADFORD CITIZEN says:—

"The excellence of his poems has been specially emphasized by his having had conferred on him the honorary degrees of M.A. and LL.D."

The MIDLAND WEEKLY NEWS says:—

" He is an author and poet of considerable distinction. His poems have appeared in our columns and have met with a good deal of well-deserved praise. Wherever his works are published he wins popularity, for he is a charming singer in the poetical firmament, who must make headway in society where true poetry is best admired."

The DEWSBURY CHRONICLE says:—

" As a mark of their appreciation of his high literary attainments, the Members of the West Riding Literary Club, of which he is the founder and first President, have presented him with a valuable life sized portrait of himself."

The BLACKBURN DAILY TELEGRAPH says:—

" Dr. Forshaw's poems exhibit genuine poetic feeling. They are smoothly and gracefully written, and his verse is generally musical."

PRESS OPINIONS

ON THE

Poets of Keighley, Bingley & District.

Edited by CHAS. F. FORSHAW, LL.D.

The BRADFORD OBSERVER says :—

"Some of the best work of the poets and versifiers who have lived and sung in that part of the valley of the Aire where the above towns are situated and in its near neighbourhood is collected in this book. The editor has performed his task in a catholic and tolerant spirit. Short but sufficient biographies of the various authors are given. Whilst the collection has value as a record of local talent, it subserves a useful purpose in preserving for reference many fugitive fragments of verse which would otherwise have been lost to the general reader."

The YORKSHIRE POST says :—

"A valuable work, splendidly edited, and neatly and carefully printed."

The LEEDS MERCURY says :—

"Dr. Forshaw has produced a work of considerable local interest. The work is carefully edited, and Dr. Forshaw is to be congratulated on the appearance of what is an acceptable addition to our Yorkshire anthology."

The YORKSHIREMAN says :—

"Dr. Forshaw has been more than usually fortunate in his selections."

The BINGLEY CHRONICLE says :—

"A neat volume of biography and poetry. The examples are very well selected, and altogether the book is an exceedingly creditable and interesting production, besides being useful in its purpose. In its own neighbourhood at least it should be a great success."

The HECKMONDWIKE HERALD says :—

"Those who love the poet's "Wild Imaginings" will, we are sure, be pleased with this little book. It contains specimens of gifted writers, and each selection is prefaced by well written biographies which are by no means the least interesting portions of the book. It is well got up and is a credit to both editor and publishers."

The BRADFORD TELEGRAPH says:

"Dr. Forshaw has brought out an attractive volume dealing with poets whose names locally are familiar as household words. Brief selections from their works are prefaced in each instance by short biographical sketches, in the preparation of which several well-known local gentlemen have co-operated. In several instances original portraits and illustrations are given. The book is notable as a successful local instance of the co-operative system of bookmaking now so much in favour. Dr. Forshaw has done his editing well, and the book is worthy of the attention of those interested in the study of local literature."

The KEIGHLEY HERALD says:—

"An interesting and fascinating volume. The type is distinct and clear, the paper good, and the numerous illustrations well executed. Dr. Forshaw has collated his materials with scrupulous care—the perusal of the pages has afforded us much pleasure, and we heartily commend the volume to our readers as an honest effort to bring our local poets into due prominence amongst the *litterateurs* of the county."

The BRADFORD MERCURY says:—

"The biographical sketches of the various. persons who are dealt with in the book are particularly interesting."

The SKIPTON PIONEER says:—

"Some of the poems are admirable."

The BRIGHOUSE NEWS says:—

"The poems are selected with good judgment and form an admirable collection. A very good feature of the book is that several of the biographies are written by well known literary men. The book is one which does credit to both author and publishers, and we have pleasure in recommending it to the notice of our literary readers."

The DEWSBURY CHRONICLE says:—

"The biographies are written by all the leading local literary lights of the day. With Dr. Forshaw's enterprise and enthusiasm the book was bound to go."

The HULL CRITIC says:—

"The contributions do much credit to the literary doctor."

The LONDON ASSOCIATE says:—

"Dr. Forshaw has shown not only appreciation, but discrimination as well, in his treatment of the poets of Keighley and its locality. The work is well and copiously illustrated, and the letterpress is everything that could be desired. The quality of the poems, too, is considerably above the average.

Press Opinions on 'Yorkshire Poets, Past & Present'

Edited by CHAS. F. FORSHAW, LL.D.

This work is now in its fifth volume, and comprises biographies, with
examples of the poetry, of over five hundred
Yorkshire versifiers—

Price per vol. 5/- bound in half calf.

The BRADFORD DAILY TELEGRAPH says:—

"Yorkshire Poets, past and present,' edited by Dr. Forshaw, has
for its aim to provide a complete book of reference to Yorkshire
poetry. The work will be rather onerous and a great deal will depend
on the judicious selection of the extracts. So far as judgment can
be formed from the parts before us (the first six) the Editor appears
likely to attain a marked degree of success, and if the future numbers
are equal to these 'Yorkshire Poets' may safely be commended to all
interested in the literary achievements of the county of broad acres."

The DEWSBURY CHRONICLE says:—

"We have received from Dr. Forshaw the first three numbers of
'Yorkshire Poets,' of which that gentleman is the able editor. The
poems are pieces of pleasant rhythm and sympathetic sentiment. We
should like to hear of this neat and attractive publication commanding
a very wide sale."

The LEEDS TIMES says:—

"Dr. Forshaw, whose devotion to the muse is well known, has
brought out a monthly serial under the title of 'Yorkshire Poets, past
and present,' consisting of the writings of Yorkshire poets and short
biographical sketches. These selections are made with much taste and
judgment and are gems of great beauty. The serial is is well printed
and has been most favourably received all over Yorkshire. We con-
gratulate Dr. Forshaw on the commencement of what promises to be
a most interesting and valuable work—the collection and arrangement
as a whole is worthy of all praise. A poet himself of no mean order,
the task of editing such a work as this comes quite *con amore* to
Dr. Forshaw."

The HULL EXPRESS says:—

"Dr. Forshaw is not only a poet but a prolific prose writer—his
work on 'Yorkshire Poets, past and present,' promises to be of great
literary interest, and is tastefully printed and published. We wish
Dr. Forshaw much success in his undertaking—he has evidently a
tremendous task before him."

The WAKEFIELD HERALD says:—

"To those interested in the highest branch of literature the
magazine will prove a good book of reference, besides supplying many
a happy hour's reading."

The PUDSEY DISTRICT ADVERTISER says:—

"An interesting publication, neatly and carefully printed, which should become popular, and possesses a noteworthy feature which ought to render it specially valuable as a work of reference. We refer to the information it will supply with respect to the births and deaths of past poets, and of the births of living poets when obtainable. We wish success to this new literary undertaking."

The HULL ARROW says:—

"An excellent little pamphlet of selections from 'Yorkshire Poets, past and present.' The poems given thoroughly prove Dr. Forshaw's artistic preception in selecting them for his delightful penny-worth of art."

The BRIGHOUSE NEWS says:—

"Seems likely to prove an attractive and popular work. We hope Dr. Forshaw will long continue this labour of love in the interest of all Yorkshiremen."

The BARNSLEY CHRONICLE says:—

"Dr. Forshaw has already made his mark as a lecturer and an author, and has given ample evidence for his fitness to edit a series of 'Yorkshire Poets.' The facts, dates, etc. given are strictly reliable, and the selections have in all cases been judiciously made. The task Dr. Forshaw has set himself is a laudable one, and we shall have pleasure in directing attention to the work from time to time as it progresses."

The MIDLAND OBSERVER says:—

"The standard and high class quality of the carefully-edited work increases with the appearance of each number. The selected poems are all of exceptional merit, and possess a general excellence that proclaims for Yorkshire poetry a high position in the poetical world. We can only add that the successful conduct of the newly-printed poetic serial in the hands of Dr. Forshaw is a sufficient guarantee that the contents will afford both pleasure and profit to lovers of the muse. To those who have not perused this album of poetic gems, we advise the obtaining of a current number and appreciation must follow."

The EASTERN MORNING NEWS says:

"The numbers improve as they go on. It will be valuable and interesting as a book of reference, as the editor intends to make it very exhaustive, and to include every Yorkshire writer of any note who has committed the sinfulness of a sonnet, the transgression of a trochee, the iniquity of an iambic, or even the crime of a couplet."

The NORTHERN DAILY TELEGRAPH says:..

"The editor is doing full justice to the subject and his work should find a ready appreciation amongst Yorkshiremen."

The WHARFEDALE OBSERVER says:—

"Dr. Forshaw not only possesses literary ability, but true poetic taste. Amongst Yorkshiremen the publication should have a large sale."

To be Published in December, 1891, by

THORNTON & PEARSON, 17, Barkerend Road, Bradford.

—➤⦂◦⦂◄—

THE

Poets of the Spen Valley,

(ILLUSTRATED).

Edited by CHARLES F. FORSHAW, LL.D.

Price to Subscribers, 2/-.   Non-Subscribers, 3/6 nett.

Being Poems and Biographies of various Natives and Residents of Birkenshaw, Birstall, Cleckheaton, Heckmondwike, Liversedge, Wyke, and Neighbourhood.

Many of the leading Authors of the day will contribute the Biographical Sketches, amongst whom will be HERBT. SHACKLETON, M.R.C.S. L.R.C.P.I. JOSEPH GAUNT, B.A. W. J. KAYE, M.A. and Rev. Dr. RIX.

The Volume will be got up in a similar style to "The Poets of Keighley, Bingley, and District," and is one of a series which Dr. Forshaw purposes issuing—and he hopes to deal with every district in Yorkshire in a like manner, completing the work in twenty volumes.

The following is list of some of the Authors who will appear in the Book :—

ETHEL BIRKBY,	CHARLOTTE OATES,
EDITH M. BRIGGS,	JOHN ODDY,
HERBERT KNOWLES,	HARRIET GARSIDE,
WILLIAM WRIGHT,	H. C. DANIELS,
JONAS BRIGGS,	W. NAYLOR.

IN ACTIVE PREPARATION

And will shortly be published by THORNTON & PEARSON, of Bradford, in one volume. Crown 8vo. Boards. 300 pp. Price 3/-.

The Poetesses of Yorkshire

Edited by

CHAS. F. FORSHAW, LL.D. D.D.S.

This is a work that Dr. Forshaw has been engaged on for some years past—its conception is entirely original, no other similar work having appeared in Yorkshire or elsewhere.

The Biographers will be men of eminence in the Literary World.

Amongst the Authoresses dealt with will be the following:

Maria Arthington,	Eliza C. Green,	Mrs. E. M. Perring,
Mrs. A. S. Bell,	Alice Haley,	Mrs. S. K. Phillips,
Mrs. R. H. Bilsborough,	Beulah K. Hanson,	Elizabeth Platt,
Ethel Birkby,	Hon. Anabella Hawk,	Amy Dora Reynolds,
Emma Battye,	Lady Hawkshaw,	Charlotte Richardson,
Edith M. Briggs,	Mrs. R. Hey,	Charlotte C. Richardson,
Anne Brontë,	E. G. Hodgson,	Mary Roberts.
Charlotte Brontë,	Barbara Hofland,	E. F. A. Sergeant,
Emily J. Brontë,	Patty Honeywood,	Maria Shackleton,
Mrs. Jane Bruce,	Louisa A. Horsfield,	Jane Shackleton,
Annie Carey,	Mary Hutton,	Elizabeth Slights,
Mary A. E. Charnock,	T. F. B. Jackson,	Octavia Stopford,
Maria Cliffe,	F. M. H. Kaye,	Jane G. Sutherland,
Annie Clough,	Jane Kidd,	Mrs. Sutcliffe,
Miss Dickinson,	Mary Masters,	Lucy Ann Thorne,
Grace Dickinson,	Mrs. Merryweather,	Elizabeth Tweddell,
Frances E. Dunlop,	Mrs. Ann Moss,	Sarah Wilcock,
Primogene Duvard,	Emma Norman,	Eliza Wilkinson,
M. J. Elliot,	Charlotte Oates,	Julia Willoughby,
Harriet Garside,	Sarah Pearson,	Shirley Wynne,

And several anonymous writers.

*Will shortly be issued in one volume, Demy Octavo, 304 pp.,
bound in Cloth and Gold. 6/- nett.*

The Leading Poets of Scotland

FROM EARLY TIMES.

(ILLUSTRATED).

Being short Biographies and Selections from the writings of the
most eminent Scottish Bards.

EDITED BY

WALTER J. KAYE, M.A.

TRINITY COLLEGE, DUBLIN*

About seventy Poets will be dealt with, and the Biographical
Sketches will be contributed by some of our leading Authors, and
the work will be rendered more especially valuable to those interested
in Yorkshire Literature by the fact that the life sketches will be
written by well-known Yorkshire litterateurs, amongst whom will
be the following :—

REV. CANON WEST.
  ,, S. H. PARKES, B.A. F.R.A.S.
  ,, JAMES GABB, B.A.
  ,, A. H. RIX, LL.D. F.G.S.
  ,, DR. KAYE, M.A.
  ,, MORRIS GRIFFITH, B.A.
DANIEL MOORE, M.A.
DR. CHAS. F. FORSHAW, M.A.
THOS. JOHNSTONE, M.D. M.R.C.P.
THOS. WILMOT, M.R.C.S. L.R.C.P.
CLARENCE FOSTER, M.R.C.S.
HERBERT SHACKLETON, M.R.C.S. L.R.C.P.
GEORGE ACKROYD, J.P.
M. H. COCHRANE, Ph.D. F.C.S.
FREDERICK ROSS, F.R.H.S.
J. POTTER BRISCOE, F.R.H.S.
DR. JOSEPH NIX CUTTS.
JOSEPH JAMES, D.Sc.
JOSEPH GAUNT, B.A. B.Sc. F.S.A.
WILLIAM HOBSON, F.R.A.S.

*Principal of Ilkley College, Yorkshire, to whom all communications may be addressed.

Thornton & Pearson, Printers, 17, Barkerend Road, Bradford.